THE OLD ONE

THE OLD ONE

David Middlebrook

URION PRESS

Copyright © 1973 by the

ᴗrion press
P.O. Box 2244
Eugene, Oregon 97402

SBN Hardcover: 913522-01-5
SBN Paperback: 913522-02-3
Library of Congress Catalog
Card Number: 73-80996

*Back cover and frontispiece by
John Pittman
Front cover drawing by
Margaret Matson*

Printed in U.S.A.

the old one

All changed
Changed utterly,
A terrible beauty is born

YEATS

Active virtue is learning
to love and understand your
opposite

I

In the dark of his room, Peter looked at the curvy luminous hands of the watch he had been given for his tenth birthday. The cartoon face at the center grinned and the improbable shoots which formed the time said three o'clock. He stepped out of bed, pulled his pants on over his pajamas, put on his T-shirt and jacket. Then, pinching the tops of his boots between his fingers, he tiptoed into the hall. His soft shinbone hurt where his father had kicked him the evening before. His mother slept in the next room in a single bed while his father lay at the end of the hall on the army cot he had brought back with him from the war in 1953. The double bed which man and wife once used leaned against the wall in the garage; it had caved in beneath the exertions of one hundred situps, twenty-five leglifts - the daily trouble of an ex-soldier whose civilian job drove him to the revenge of exercise - secondary revenge against his wife.

The screen door croaked briefly as Peter opened it and crept down the front steps. Shepp and his friends would be walking through the dark town now on their way to Tot's. Peter sat on the bottom step and pulled on his boots. He shivered though it was not cold.

The treeless street looked menacing in the inquisitive glare of the streetlamps. The avenue itself, like the other avenues of the town, was so straight that a blindman could walk it if someone pointed him in the right direction.

He stood up and tread on the sparse lawns, avoiding the sidewalk. Soon he passed the house where his friend Arthur had once lived. It seemed impossible to him that the house had not vanished along with his friend, and he looked carefully. Beyond the car parked in the driveway he could see a light burning in the garage.

Arthur had been different from anyone now living in the town of Shays. He had been like a window through which Peter could view the blood-red apples and blue mountains of a mirthful adventurous life. Not many of the other people in town had known about their friendship or felt the same way about Arthur. In fact, some individuals who did not even know Peter had made it impossible for Arthur's parents to continue to live in Shays and the family had left town.

In the two years since Arthur had moved away, Peter had come to love Tot, even though an older boy, Shepp, loved her too.

A dog began to bark. Peter hurried his pace and glanced behind him. No light flashed through the windows, but the dog's voice followed him, becoming less distinct and strange in the quiet.

Tot's house with frayed telephone wires hanging behind it, appeared like a giant, seated in the night with his hat off. The others were not there yet. Somewhere within, Peter knew, she must be tossing, putting on her clothes, or watching from her window. He crouched down within the dry twigs of a bush, watching alternately the front and rear of the house.

Then he heard the tread of feet. Shepp and his two friends, Chase and Randolph, were shadows bobbing along the fence which Tot's mother had carefully strung with bell-shaped flowers. The shadows came back, then with a crash, settled not four feet from Peter. He wanted to announce himself with a frightening yell. But he knew Shepp would not even be thinking about him. Shepp was probably wondering what he would find out at the mines.

But what if Peter took out the knife in his pocket and slashed the throat of his enemy and left him chalk-white in the bush? Then Tot and Peter would be free. Together they would travel to a distant town. Peter would have to find work. He would go to a restaurant where the sign, 'Bus-boy Needed', would be taped to a window. But the man behind the counter would look at Peter knowingly. His hands, resting on the counter, would be chalk-white and the man would see Peter's ghost-white face and the ashamed face of Tot.

Now Peter watched her come out of the house. She walked toward the street, tucking something under her jacket.

The bush snapped and the other boys hurried on tiptoe into the middle of the avenue. Peter waited. He could easily recognize his enemy whose size and large curving hat were like trademarks. One day in winter, a cowboy had passed through town, riding on horseback among the cars and shoppers. Shepp had made a bargain with the cowboy, saying that he would give him anything for his hat. The little man had put the hat on Shepp's head and continued on without once looking back. Peter, watching it all, had cursed Shepp for taking the gift, especially since it was not given out of friendship, but because Shepp was a grabber.

He waited until the quartet was far in advance, then he followed.

They walked down the very center of the highway

which entered the town from the East. Manikins stood in the windows of a dry-goods store. The record store and the creamery were silent. The electricity droned and crackled in the pale streetlamps.

Within a few minutes, the youths were outside the town. Its eastern end stopped suddenly with a gas station and a sign saying, Shays pop. 15,000. Then the desert thickened, the sky darkened and the stars came out; and the little clump of city lay behind them like a stage set.

On the other end of town, the western end, the city extended - as though yearning for the ever-distant blueness of the sea. It was in this area of town that box-shaped glass and aluminum buildings were being constructed; banks which cheered up electrical companies and those borrowers who, in view of the few businesses that had come to Shays, were willing to stay on. The mines which the old Southerner named Shay had worked were boarded up in the hillsides now. According to Peter's father, the future of the town depended on the new businesses, and the big plant that punched out plastic parts for sewing machines and kitchen gadgets. Brochures had been printed up and sent to people all over the country, promising a commercial future. for Shays that would be hard to guarantee on the basis of its clapboard appearance.

To a small extent, the new section proved that Shays could do it. For the children, the walls of the structures provided good surfaces on which to write slogans. The stores were easy to steal from despite the mirrors inside which were supposed to stop the fun. Most of the time, the children moved in restless groups, wondering what excitement was in store, or evil – filling in the gaps.

The darkness – though it served as a cover for the thirteen-year-old Peter – forced him to draw closer. Scud, scud, scud went the steps in front of him. Once when the steps stopped, he dropped flat. A flame was ignited and four faces poked cigarettes at the lighter which Shepp had taken from his father's drawer.

Soon the road was abandoned for a dirt track which led to the mines.

It was still dark.

The others were talking about Mrs. Lawson who wore tight sweaters in social studies class, put her feet up on the desk and left school every day with a different man. They wondered if she knew that boys fought for the front seats so they could look up her dress. They next speculated about what their mothers and fathers did in bed at night and what spying, if any, had been done. The rival town close to Shays, Silverton, had a good basketball team. The big Chinese center who had flunked two grades could murder anyone in the desert. Then they wondered about the punishments which would be coming to them when their parents found out about their adventure. Chase, who had slept over at Randolph's house, didn't have to worry. He described some punishments he had received in the past so that the others wouldn't resent his freedom. Parents so seldom speak about what their real desires and wants are, that almost anything could be expected of them. So it was throw water into the wind, it didn't matter.

Peter tried to imagine things that would terrify

the noisy band ahead of him: crying, the thuds and gruntings of a beast, conversation in a feigned voice. What kind of voice would scare them? It would have to be cracked and old. He would creep up close to them and say, "Pecos, ya hear 'em, you hear that? Kids." Nothing more. They would pause. A short conference; they'd run. He would chase them, tearing at brush, throwing dust and rocks, swearing in a foreign burst of sounds, making the desert clamor with the yells of a maddened soul.

His quarrel with Shepp had gone on for some time. It had started the day Peter got up the fire to go over to Tot's house. He had hunted around in his drawer for a gift of some kind. All he could find was a Valentine's card his Aunt in Wisconsin had sent him the preceding year. It had a soft red cushion on the front of it, with bows. He changed the To and From, erased some pencil marks, and in a few minutes, was pressing it into Tot's grateful hands. Then Shepp had swung up the path.

"Chewed-up gum, you're such an actor that your nose is blue, you piece of vine with hair growing on it." Peter had raged on with the insults until he couldn't think of any more.

"Who's this?" Shepp had asked.

"Peter."

"You look like a diddy-doo; what did you call me all the names for?"

Because I knew you'd say I looked stupid."

"Heh." Shepp screwed up his eyes and nose and looked down at him.

"Do you like Squirt?"

"No."

"Tot and I are going to have a Squirt."

Tot cocked her head at the younger boy. He sat with his chin on his knees. Then in a kind of slow motion she walked to where Shepp waited, still looking back at him.

The next time Peter spoke with Shepp the other boy didn't try to be so friendly. He was standing in front of the creamery with four or five of his friends. He said "Hi," and stepped in Peter's way.

"What?" Peter asked.

"That's a big coat you have on." Peter's jacket –

made of a soft grey material, with white snaps, hung halfway to his knees. It was reversible with pointed pockets at the bottom.

"It doesn't have hair on it."

Shepp twitched and looked at his own jacket as if to make sure his didn't either. Then his eyes squinted.

"Listen, we're going to go to the supply shop and get some stuff. Help us now, we'll give you some of it."

"You wouldn't give me a thing."

"I said we would. Don't you believe me?"

"I don't like to steal."

"Chuckle, chuckle, diddy-doo," said Shepp.

The other boys snickered.

It was late. There weren't many people in the street, and Peter wanted to get home. On the other side of the road, a kind of freak, who nevertheless, was familiar to everyone at the school, had set himself up as a spectator. People said he had cooties. Shepp and the others who were immune to the cooties could tell who had them and who didn't. Now the attention of the odd youth was fixed on Peter and

Shepp. He gave a loud rasping laugh. His eyes seemed to have been boiled; whenever he talked, his teeth would make a strange clicking noise. No one had ever mentioned that there was a resemblance between Peter and this creature, but as far as Peter could judge, they looked alike. He was sure that Shepp would point out the resemblance any minute and the others would agree; but for some reason, it didn't occur to Shepp. The tall boy pretended he hadn't even heard the laugh from across the street. Peter took a step to the side.

"What do you want?"

"If you don't like to steal," Shepp continued, "then what are you doing with Tot all the time?"

Peter didn't answer.

"That's the little man's way," said Randolph, who stood next to Chase. Randolph's face was sweating; his fingers dragged a comb through his long red hair.

Peter's tongue, usually so ready, clotted. Tot was such a secret that in his own heart she lived within a kind of plastic tent sealed off from everything else. It had never occurred to him that she meant something to Shepp. Shepp was just a threat, a presence. But as Peter stood on the sidewalk with Shepp breathing on him, just a few inches from his body, he could hardly ignore him.

"Watch yourself, diddy-doo," said Shepp. Then he stepped aside.

Later that month, Peter had showed up at a basketball game. But before he went into the gym, he stood outside about a hundred yards from where the noise of the game met the sky through the glass roll-away top of the auditorium – pressing his hand against a red box with sharp corners and a glass eye – wondering if the box had a voice. He was perfectly hidden; the driver education building was dark, but the fire alarm, if set off there, would have the same effect as if pulled within the auditorium itself. He could not help thinking of the little box as a person, with a little bell inside. He did not want to hear a smothered metallic voice as he ran away. There were two sounds: first the pop of glass, then a brilliant alarm inside the building.

He ran along the asphalt, whirling once to look behind him. With his breath coming warm from between his teeth, he entered through one of the gym doors. He spotted Shepp and Tot and took a seat directly across the court from them.

Inside, the air was hot, deafened with echoes and shouts, the floor waxed like a mirror and filled with the reflected light of a thousand bulbs enclosed in wire cages. The rubber sneakers on the feet of the players made pinched shrieks; the players changed directions, then ran back and forth the length of the court, the ball booming against the polished floor. From time to time the referee froze the boys and made them wait for his toss.

Shepp and Tot did not notice Peter for at least five minutes. By that time the quarter was about to end; the first fireman, lifting his eyes to look every whichway, sniffing, ran in through one of the doors with an axe under his arm. Five or six others came in through side entrances but the referee didn't blow his whistle. One of the firemen walked into the action, and the Silverton team, about to score another basket, declared unfair play. The big Chinese center who had control of the ball, smashed it down on the floor and swaggered up to the fireman.

In the echoing chaos of shouting spectators and players, Peter hurried around the upper tier of the gym. Shepp had joined some of his friends in an advance on the floor, leaving Tot behind.

"Do you want to know who did it?" Peter said to an enormous fireman who was checking under the bleachers.

"Some kid pull the alarm?"

"That one." Peter pointed to the descending form of Shepp, "with the black coat on."

"I see him." The fireman wheezed and jumped clumsily down the stairs.

Peter hurried around the walkway and down the wooden tiers to where Tot sat watching Shepp's hat. He leaned down in back of her and whispered in her ear.

"I was the one who did it."

She turned and smiled. "What did you do?"

"I just pulled the fire alarm to make Shepp get

lost."

Her face flushed. As she jumped up, she leaned on him and hurried to step over the seat.

"You must have felt terrible, that's why," she explained.

Despite the turbulence of his feelings, he did not feel terrible. A sense of doom about the whole project, though, had troubled him even before he had left his house. Now as he pushed her before him through the door, that sense was confirmed. Shepp had caught sight of Peter running up the stairs with Tot and was pointing him out to the fireman, asking him something. The fireman nodded.

"Guess what," Peter said to Tot. "I'm caught."

"What will they do?" she asked.

He took her hand. "Give me the works."

They ran while a siren, approaching from a different direction, signalled the arrival of another firetruck. Her white socks beneath her dark blue pants flashed in the darkness.

They ran down two alleys, then stopped. She was panting hard.

"Don't go back," she said.

"Go back there? What for?"

"Maybe I should, though."

"You didn't do anything," Peter said.

"I mean because of Shepp. He's going to be mad at you."

"More than that. I told a fireman that Shepp set off the alarm."

"Oh," she said. "You'd better come to my house."

They set off at a fast walk, but just as they turned the corner of her street, Shepp – his arms and legs all crazy with his pace – jolted to a halt in front of them.

"Well, there's a problem," he announced, catching his breath, "and the firemen want to talk to you about it." He pointed with his outstretched arm, as though ordering Peter from a tract of land. He dropped his arm and panted, biting at the air as it came through his teeth. "You better find out about it."

"O.K."

"You better find out about it," said Shepp again, stepping closer to Peter. "Don't play your tricks on

- 17 -

me. They wanted to take me down to the station. You yellow belly, they'll have you pegged in a minute. Go talk to them, go talk to them."

Peter almost wished that Shepp had knocked him down.

"So I'm a crook, right?"

"That's right, that's right."

"So are you."

Shepp nodded. "Go on, yellow belly."

Peter turned and retraced his steps. He walked halfway down the alley, then ran around the block and went home.

As he lay in bed, the air seemed thronged with bright and dark shapes; the shapes moved restlessly and wound him within themselves as he tossed in his bedclothes, trying to sleep. They were powerful speaking things – many and powerful.

Two days passed, then he was called into the superintendent's office. Mrs. Bright and the fireman faced him.

"Did you pull the alarm, Peter?"

"Yes."

His father arrived and his reaction was what Peter had expected it to be. His anger went on for months, feeding on itself because it was stored up. The harangues lasted longer than the man's emotions could actually sustain them. So the same question was asked over and over. "Do you know, do you know what you've done?" Peter's idea was better than his father's. Kicked previously for his slowness and secretiveness, now he was punished because he had entered the circle of pranksters which just months before had seemed like noble savages to his father. The ex-corporal from the beginning had either misunderstood or never known the motives of a healthy prankster.

Peter's mother absolved herself from the creature who had stretched her life with so many ins and outs – not the least of which was his becoming, in her words, "an arsonist".

But on the firechief rested the burden of Peter's reform. "He'd probably enjoy the hell out of the fires, so don't take him to any of those," the Chief said to a rookie named Frank, who was going to be Peter's work-supervisor. "Let him polish the trucks and take him out on inspection."

Peter really didn't enjoy the fires. They couldn't compare with the blazing cities he had seen on television with everything charred looking, and small people coming slowly away with white staring eyes. He dutifully polished the trucks, though, and even liked to clean the giant headlamps. On his car rides with Frank, he became accustomed to the smell of ashes – the wetness of abject decay.

One day Peter asked him why he had become a fireman.

"Want to know?" Frank grinned and flicked his front tooth with his fingernail. "I accidentally blowtorched a kid in metalshop."

Peter gulped. "You did!"

"Forget it, no, no. Don't get excited."

"You did!"

Peter couldn't get the idea out of his head. It led ultimately to an idea about Shepp. A blowtorch was an arc, a blue light – irredeemable. It changed as though a different world had visited the thing it touched. A burned house was nothing compared to it. The house would have to turn into a toad if the effect were to be visualized.

Shepp had instructed Tot never to speak to Peter. She could not give him sympathy of any kind over the phone. In the older boy's mind, Tot encouraged Peter merely out of feminine sympathy. He could not imagine that Peter had any real hold on her.

But Peter's experiences with Frank and the men at the fire station delighted her. Despite his punishments and beatings, he was dauntless. He paid more attention to her and was more thoughtful than Shepp by far. Messages from him appeared under her doorsill and in her locker, also little gifts and monstrous tales, some humorous, about Shepp. For these stories, she criticized him.

At Easter time, the regional supply company of which Peter's father was manager, arranged a trip down to the Texas coast and Peter went along. He returned healthy and brown with the ragged sores on his fingers closed over and healed by swimming and the sun. But within a month he looked almost the

- 21 -

same again. His hands were bitten by teeth which worked industriously in the night. His coloring flaked and left his face motley.

Then one day, Tot told Peter she had to go with Shepp on a hike, in the middle of the night, and this made Peter furious.

So, not long after the horizon began to fill up with hot yellow light and Peter had stalked for two hours in the darkness, Shepp turned around and spied Peter following at a distance.

The boarded-up mines were just visible like little crosses on the hillside as Shepp plucked Tot's jacket. The rival stood about seventy-five yards away like a spectre in the dawn. He was no longer trying to hide.

"Well, what's he doing here?" Shepp asked Tot.

Randolph and Chase showed clean hands. Chase was slow to get angry about anything, though Randolph was already boiling.

"This is the limit." Shepp took off his hat and punched his fist into it again and again, being careful not to puncture the felt.

"The whole thing's spoiled," he said.

"He won't bother us," Tot assured him.

"You're right. You're right. He has to turn around, that's what, and he has to go back now."

"Why? He's just following, don't get mad at him," said Tot. "I was the one, I told him. Now are you going to be mad at me?" She looked down at the toe of her saddle shoe while she pushed dust over pebbles.

"I said I don't want you to talk to him!" Shepp put his hat back on his head and began to walk toward Peter.

The darkness had provided Peter with good hiding as he pursued his enemy beneath the thick stars. But the fierce bits of light were gone now. The day shut out all but the sage, clinging in whirled shapes to the dust, and hills that looked like grey sea waves behind them.

A single prayer failed to take hold in Peter's head. He was determined to be recognized. But as he watched the form of Shepp approaching him, he thought of all the gods he had ever heard of. He prayed to Jesus of Nazareth, Buddha, and the

Rain-god. Finally, he thought of the miraculous batteries in his flashlight at home which had not burned out in six years. But all of this was not apparent to Shepp. Peter looked as resolute as a deadly bandit.

"Nice surprise," said Shepp, coming to a halt in front of him.

"No surprise."

"What is it, then? I know, you must have a hide-away you intend to run off to with Tot." Shepp laughed. "You won't get the chance, because you have to turn around and go back."

"Piece of dust, bellywart," muttered Peter.

"What did you say?" Shepp put his hands on his hips and leaned forward as if to hear better.

"Tot should be able to do anything she wants to. You're not her ruler."

"Heh." Shepp took off his hat and scratched his head. "Hokay, let me figure. You want me to let Tot do anything she wants. You expect me to let her walk around town with a yellow belly and make a freak out of herself and mama you anytime you want and not have me say anything about it. I see." Shepp put his hat back on.

"That's right," said Peter.

"But it isn't going to work that way," said Shepp. "You don't work, get it?"

"I'm not supposed to. One day, you're going to die a fast death."

"Is that so? Swami, heh? Those were your last words."

Shepp took off his jacket. He lay it on the ground and put his hat on top of it. He did this with great ceremony. Then he rolled up his sleeves. There on his arms were the hairs that so distinguished him. The wooly covering looked strange on the arms of a fifteen-year-old boy. Like a sadistic comment on the part of nature, they grew wild and upstanding.

"Are you going to go back?"

Shepp made it clear that this was his ultimatum.

"Rule of the big arms, that's you," said Peter. He narrowed his eyes and blinked. His fists were crossed in front of his chest and he looked like a little Egyptian Pharaoh. His Aunt had once said that there was a jewel inside of a person. Now he wished that it were on his chin so it would cut the fist of his enemy.

Shepp took special care. He stepped slowly around the little idol-man, then began to pace back and forth, increasing his speed and pumping his arms up and down like locomotive rods. At one point, to Peter's mind, Shepp in fact looked like a locomotive churning across the desert with a glinting sun rising behind him.

Then there were stars, yellow circles, and a buzzing noise like a locust. When he thought it was safe, Peter opened his eyes again. Shepp had re-joined the group and they were moving away. Peter pressed the place where he had been hit. A little knot was swelling on his forehead. He felt himself all over. While he was still in a sitting position, he took off his jacket. He stood up and tied the sleeves around his waist; then he followed, thinking, "If he hits me again his arm will fall off."

"You shouldn't have hurt him," said Tot.

"Why not? If you hadn't told him where we were

going he wouldn't have followed and he wouldn't have gotten the mash."

"That's right," said Randolph. Shepp doesn't have any choice. Peter should have gotten it a long time ago."

"It won't do any good," said Tot.

As they walked, Randolph and Chase picked targets and threw their pegknives. Quick lizards sought cover in the brush. And occasionally, they could see a snake moving in the alleyways of dust.

"See?" said Tot. She stopped and pointed.

The figure of Peter came to a halt about two-hundred yards behind.

"He's crazy, he doesn't know what he's doing and Shepp will have to give it to him again," said Randolph. "Listen, we'll have a good old time with him in the mines."

"You ought to forget about Peter," she said. "And how are we going to get into the mines?" Tot motioned to the boarded-up entrances not far distant.

"We won't hurt him," Shepp said, picking up a handful of dirt. He threw it; then he turned and walked up the incline, followed by the others. He whirled on her suddenly. "Do you want to go with him? Go on, go home."

"No," she said.

Underfoot, bits of wood and broken tools came into view. An abandoned orecart stood in the sand rusting on a track that ended almost as soon as it began. The wind had blown tides of dust in front of the entryways. The mines which had once nurtured the body and soul of Shays, were closed to visitors.

"Locks." Chase pulled at the metal latches. A wire gate behind the boards was locked in three places.

Shepp kicked at the barrier. "Well," he said. He found the head of a pickaxe. "We can get rid of the boards anyway." He began to use the tool like a crowbar on the slats. The two friends searched around for other implements.

Tot sat down on a rock and watched. Peter was watching too, from a distance, on another rock.

Tot imagined all kinds of harm that could come to him. But there they were, three boys tearing at a barrier and all they'd probably find would be a load of snakes. It was her fault. If she hadn't liked both Shepp and Peter the trouble wouldn't have started. Why Shepp thought she was worth the trouble she could only imagine. Maybe it was because she didn't nag at him, didn't expect presents, and didn't make an issue of his friendship when he was with other boys. Also, she would do almost anything he asked her to. She was like his obedient servant. But with Peter, it was different. For a long time he had been merely watchful, as though he suspected she were turning the slow axle of summer. And she had come to like him better than Shepp, even though she did not naturally obey him.

Now she wanted to find a way to divert them all. The side of the mine entrance was close by. They didn't notice when she disappeared behind it and began to run up the slope.

Peter assumed she was trying to find a spot where she could go to the bathroom. This is what the other boys thought too when they noticed she was gone. But after ten minutes Shepp dropped his tool and walked around the side of the mine. He shouted her name up the hill.

"What's going on?" he said. Chase and Randolph joined him. The three of them shouted her name.

Peter stood up too, and listened. The May sun had moved into the sky like a lobster. What crackled in the air, in the silent desert, with the heat and the stillness? Peter looked with mistrust at the stationary ore cart, the mine, and the hills themselves. The three boys ahead moved quickly up the slope.

The hill was not steep. Behind it rose more hills, tier on tier, blocking out the desert floor which lay behind them.

Punch-colored rocks skittered down behind their shoes as they hurried up the second incline – less steep and longer than the first.

They were getting out of breath: it was hard to keep up the halloo and climb at the same time.

"Wait a while," said Shepp. "She must be around here somewhere."

Randolph nodded. "She has to be close by or she would have told us she was going someplace else."

Chase didn't like to talk unless he had to. He frowned at the hills that were stacked one behind the other in frozen waves.

In the area where the slope in front of them and the crest they stood on formed a kind of spillway leading to the floor of the plains, a lone yucca grew like a unique experiment on the part of a maker who could not duplicate it.

Peter was hurrying, not far behind now, a thought in his head as black as an eclipse.

All four of them heard her voice at once. It was reed-like and small, but they were upon her before they knew it.

Over her. She was about a half-story beneath them, looking up at them from a narrow pit that was shaped like a sphere. A shelf of rock protected it, hiding it from the view of anyone a short distance away. The same rock acted like a fall when potent jets of rain whistled at the earth in desert storms, sucking at and finally peeling away the stony skin of the surface.

"Well, are you hurt?" Shepp asked.

"I'm all right," she said.

Shepp examined the lip of the opening, and, on his hands and knees, stuck his head down into it. The dark air was cool; beside Tot lay a mound of rain-washed stones.

"Please," she said. "Help me out."

He took off his leather jacket. "Let's make a rope so we can climb out again." Randolph and Chase took off their jackets and began to tie them together.

Peter crept forward, dropped his jacket on the ground, glanced at Tot briefly, then hurried away.

"Now he's getting helpful," said Shepp. He took up the jacket, tied a knot in the sleeve, then pulled the sleeve through a cleft in the rocks until the knot caught. He hauled back, testing it, and then tied the other jackets to Peter's. He dropped the end of the makeshift rope into the opening.

"Get away, back up," Shepp told her. He jumped down. For about a second, he was in the air. Randolph and Chase followed.

Like the tail of an enormous kite, the jackets dangled through the opening. Tot need only climb it and join Peter; then he would jerk the tail loose and they could escape, leaving the others to live out the rest of their lives underground like moles. That would be a good punishment, Peter thought. He picked up two sharp rocks and approached the opening, peering down to see where Tot was.

"You could ride a horse in here," Chase was saying.

"Do you think it was part of the mines?" asked Randolph.

"It's a hideout," Shepp said. "Maybe the army used to put H-bombs in here. Now we have to see how far it goes." His hand fumbled in his pocket and came out with the lighter.

"Maybe Randolph's right; maybe this is a part of the mines," Tot's voice suggested.

"We hang on to one another," said Shepp, "and no talking. And that goes for when we get back. I don't care what the place turns out to be."

"Right," agreed Chase.

"Tot, do you hear?"

"I won't tell anyone," she said. Her voice was

small and she was invisible to Peter though he could see the backs and trousers of the boys. They were preparing to explore deeper.

"Don't go too fast," said Chase. He gripped Shepp by the belt.

"O.K., I'm set." Randolph gripped Chase like-wise.

Peter watched as the three boys disappeared slowly from his sight, Shepp going before with the flame. He waited for a minute, then called down,

"Psst! Tot?"

"What?"

"Grab the rope."

"What?"

"Grab it. Climb up here."

"Why?"

Peter got down on his hands and knees and tried to see her.

"They'd be stuck but good. We could steal the rope."

"They'd just boost Shepp," she said.

He listened for the voices of the boys, and hearing nothing, leaped down the hole. The impact jarred his knees.

"Where are you?"

"Here." She was sitting a few yards from the entrance, barely visible. The after-effects of the sun still blinded him. He felt around for her.

"Careful," she said.

"What's the matter?"

"I cut my knee."

"Why didn't you say so before? They would have boosted you up; then they'd be down here, and we'd be up there, up there!"

"I was the one who fell in," she said, "and all I have is this little bead chain that Chase dropped in my hair for finding the place." She pressed it into Peter's hand.

"What's wrong?" he asked. "Does your knee hurt?"

"Peter, I want to tell you something. I wanted to climb up the jackets."

"O.K., don't sit there," he said, grabbing her wrist.

"No." She pulled her hand away. "But I don't

obey you like I should."

"What do you mean?"

"Would you have stolen the jackets?"

"I would have rolled a boulder across the top too, if I could find one big enough."

"I though you meant it."

"He's going to get it; he really banged me."

"Even if I don't care about him anymore?"

Peter's head went up and down.

"You can't do the things you say you're going to. That would be no better than his hitting you."

"Much better," said Peter. Then he put his fingers to her lips. A speck of flame came into view and a soft incomprehensible blending of voices that was growing in volume in the tunnel.

He backed away, moving into the complete darkness until he knew he could not be seen.

"Aren't there any animals?" Tot asked the advancing boys.

Shepp suddenly flashed into the daylight. "Sure, lots, families, but they're all dead. Nothing to eat but the spiders. Heh."

He closed his lighter on his blue jeans and slipped it into his pocket.

"The walls are different back there," said Chase. "They're not dirt. They're smooth."

"Under your feet, too," said Randolph. He took a deep breath then added, "There's a room! The tunnel goes on, but there's a room on the left side."

"Are we going to leave now?" she asked.

"Well, you dope, of course not. But we're going to get those planks so we can see something," Shepp said.

"To make a fire with," said Chase.

"Where will the smoke go?" Tot asked.

"Get up," ordered Shepp. "What are you so worried about?"

"Peter," Randolph snorted.

"Don't get up at all," thought Peter under his breath; but watched as she did so.

"My knee's cut," she said. She showed them the little red spot on her trousers.

"That's not much." Shepp glanced at it, then waited for her to approach the jackets. As she gripped the knotted sleeves, all three of them boosted her to the surface. Then they climbed up – Shepp and Randolph dragged Chase up by the arms.

Peter advanced until he was almost at the fringe of light.

"Where's Peter?" Chase asked, inspecting the slope.

"He's still in there," said Shepp. He laughed. "Isn't that right, Peter?" he shouted down.

"That's right."

"Thought you could fool me, heh, diddy-doo?"

"No."

"Liar."

"Unless you are," said Peter. Shepp, above him, looked like a giant whose head reached through the sky. And Shepp's eyes appeared dismayed as though he didn't know what to do with the huge space he commanded. His expression became fixed again as he kneeled down on his hands and knees and lowered his head into the opening.

"C'mon, diddy-doo," he said. "Help us carry the wood."

"I have a headache," said Peter, "see?" He pointed to the bulb on his forehead.

Shepp reached his arms down. "Take hold," he said. "I'll help you." Behind Shepp, Randolph and Chase were watching Peter, their expressions impatient.

"If I took hold you'd drop me," said Peter, backing up.

"Just come on."

"I'll wait here," Peter insisted, and backed into the darkness. He turned and stumbled deeper into the passageway, but Shepp didn't follow. Peter faced around and looked at the pale spot in the darkness, waiting for them to return.

"Listen, now's the time. If I were you . . . " Randolph began.

"Just skip it, don't even have to talk about him."

They walked in silence past the yucca to the crest of the hill and down the slope.

"It isn't going to be easy carrying those planks," Chase offered. "We ought to find some little stuff to start the fire with too."

"Wait." Tot stopped, unzipped her jacket and drew out a bulging paper sack. "Do you want to eat sandwiches?" she asked. "The paper will be good for the fire."

"Hey." Shepp gave her a hug.

They took the sandwiches and began to eat hungrily. Soon they were back at the entrance to the mine.

While they were yanking the boards from the entrance, Shepp stopped his work and turned to Tot, who was sitting on the rock she had occupied before.

"Why don't you go home?" he said.

"Go home?" She sat up.

"Just go."

She took a pin from her hair and reclipped it. "You need me to carry wood, don't you? If we make two piles I can carry the end of one."

"AAhh!" He grunted. Then he struck his tool against a board and began prying again.

There were just three boards left.

Chase picked up a handful of sand and threw it at Randolph's back. Randolph stopped short and Chase leapt on his shoulders. He was carried piggyback a few yards, then both boys streaked off together toward the ore cart.

The sides of it were thin and rusty and looked as though they had been riddled by B.B. shot. The wheels and the tracks too were copper-colored and dull.

"C'mon," said Randolph.

"It won't go," said Chase.

"Let's get the sand off the tracks."

They swept the rails clean.

Randolph laughed. "Give it the works."

They braced their shoulders against the slanting metal. As they grunted and smiled, the cart – with a creak – slowly gave before them.

"Faster." Now a staccato laugh was coming from Randolph's freckled mouth. The ground began to move smoothly beneath their shoes. They were moving almost at a trot. The track curved and ended. The cart tipped, and amidst the shrieks of the boys went over at right angles with a hollow boom.

Still shrieking, they marched up the hill with

their arms over their heads. But Shepp waved them back. They ran to the sage and broke branches off. They forced some of them into their pockets. When they rejoined Shepp and Tot at the mine entrance, they fit the larger branches between the boards.

Shepp and Chase teamed up, and Tot carried with Randolph. The rough ends hurt Tot's hand, and she put her jacket bottom underneath the edges.

Walking up the hill they sang: Hi ho, O'Leary O, Hi ho, O'Leary O.

Randolph, behind Tot, kept swinging his end around like he was driving the rear section of a firetruck. As they reached the crest of the first slope, Tot turned to tell him to stop, but he swung too far and the boards clattered on the rocks, scattering the sage.

"O.K.," said Shepp. "O.K., damn it, pick 'em up. You make my hair stand on end." But he was glad to rest.

They got set again, walked down the slope and up the second hill.

After about twenty minutes, they were at the

entrance to the tunnel. They snapped the boards in half by bridging them across a rock, then they began to throw the pieces through the opening.

Peter, far back in the darkness, watched the wood flying down in the light. He knew Shepp would punish him for disobeying him, but he didn't back up. While they had been away, an idea had occurred to him. It was a daydream about Shepp. In it, Shepp was chasing Peter who had a small brother. They were running along the streets of a large city. They jumped down a manhole and found themselves in a sewer; it was a brilliant one – ornamented with glass and precious stones. Behind them, Shepp and his friends, with badges on their arms, called out to everyone to help catch Peter and his brother. "I know where we can go," Peter said. He led his brother up some stairs. They arrived in the part of the city which was devoted to churches. In one great block were all the places of worship. It was night. Peter saw a beautiful church made out of precious stones. A light was shining from the windows and at the top of the church was a cross made out of gold and fire.

"Here," said Peter. He opened the door. But inside there was only a well-lighted restaurant. There were thousands of people, but none of them would help him. He and his brother became lost in the maze of booths and eating people.

Peter waited now. He was not afraid as he had been in the daydream. If anything, he was more severe in his judgment, his determination to make Shepp pay for every wrong. He would be the spark flying from the hammer putting out the eye of the blacksmith. Somewhere, someone was writing it all down in a book. Sages would consult the book and pass it among themselves. Then Peter would come down on roller skates with wings attached and hover above them. He wouldn't say a word. They would see every point. They would close the book and praise Peter for being so patient and would work the various instruments which would seal Shepp's doom.

"If he doesn't get the point, he has to learn the old lesson," said Randolph. Shepp was the first one down the hole and now, without ceremony, was groping for Peter in the dark. The hands found him.

One hand stilled him, the other struck beneath his eye. The back of Peter's skull felt like it was on fire. He was pushed against the wall and kicked this time. He rolled up like a tightened fist and lay still. Then, into the tunnel like something still withheld, he screamed.

"Get out of the way," Shepp said to Tot who had hurried up the tunnel and crashed into him. She was holding his arms.

"What did you do to him?"

"He's not hurt. Move."

Randolph whooped.

"Where did he hurt you, Peter?" she said. But he still lay in a ball, not even sure that Shepp had gone yet. Then he sat up and leaned against the wall. He saw that Shepp had reached the entrance.

Randolph, who had taken the paper bag and wax tissue from Tot, was trying to light a fire.

"What are you lighting a fire right under the hole for?"

Randolph looked frightened. Shepp moved the wood away and scuffed out the flame. "You don't need a fire to see the light with, you dope. C'mon, grab some wood, we'll build a fire down by the room."

Chase had already set off with a few pieces. He stopped where his fingers could feel the wall becoming cool and smooth.

"Here," he said.

"O.K." Shepp dropped the wood.

They kneeled and within a few minutes, with the aid of Shepp's lighter and the kindling, the boards caught. What came into view was not the wall of an arms-cache or a mineshaft, but a pattern that might have been made by separate tides of colors had they, one by one, washed the wall with red and yellow and orange. The lines were as irregular as the mountains on an oscilloscope. They jabbed up and down and extended the distance the firelight was able to penetrate.

"Wow," Chase breathed. For a minute the other boys didn't say anything.

"Well, it was the Indians, they did this," Shepp pronounced.

"The Indians?" Chase went to the wall and moved

his finger up and down with the colors.

"Hey," said Randolph, "maybe they're still here." He jumped around in a frenzy, then ran toward the darkness and peered into it. He came back and jigged, making a high warbling sound by fluttering his hand against his mouth.

"Calm down, you idiot," said Shepp. "What's wrong with you, want to start a raid?" Already, he was swinging Randolph by the arm. Then they jumped up and down in the passageway and rammed against each other's shoulders, warbling.

"What did they use it for?" Randolph asked.

"Wait a minute. Just wait a minute," said Shepp. "Wait." He motioned over his shoulder. "Are we supposed to let Peter go back and tell everyone he wants to about this? Or what do we do?"

"Let him try it." Randolph ground his fist in his hand.

"We'd better decide about it, maybe later," said Shepp.

"How about the room?" Chase asked.

"Let's go. We'll need more wood."

They rushed back to the entrance, warbled Peter's name down the tunnel before hurrying away again.

He watched them, sitting up now, with Tot beside him.

"Just feel this one," said Peter. He took her fingers and let them touch the lump on his forehead. "Here too." Beneath his eye was a fresh bruise round with swelling. "They'd better have a good time. Whatever they get, they'll get in triple dose."

"Don't listen to them," she said. "It doesn't make any difference what they say."

"They can say anything they want to," he answered. If they beat him from morning to noon for a week they would still have to deal with the burning in his head. It was their faces, those of his enemies, which would be lighted in the flames. Sitting in the dark with Tot, and feeling her eyelashes against his cheek and her kisses, was sweet. If only she didn't kiss him all the time with her eyes open; he was glad he couldn't see her. But at the same time, he was becoming curious about their excitement.

"What do you think charged 'em up so much?"

"I don't know."

He stood up and tried to draw her to her feet. "Let's find out."

"They'll be able to see us," she said, holding back.

He looked down the tunnel. It was much longer than he had imagined it to be. The fire seemed a mile away. It had to be closer, though, because he had been able to see the boys when they were dancing. It must have been the smooth surface of the wall Chase had mentioned that had excited them. "Don't worry," Peter said. "They're thinking about something else. Now at least."

She stood up and followed him. At the entrance he handed her two pieces of wood and took some himself. The fire had been made too large, and most of the wood was gone. The wood was dry and didn't smoke much, but the sage had smoked and their eyes burned as they approached the lighted wall. They gazed at it for a minute.

"This is funny," said Peter.

"What?"

"Something."

"What's wrong?"

He told her the day-dream he had about the sewer and the colored stones. "But I didn't get caught," he added.

"Dreams are things you hope will happen some-day," she said, "and you didn't want that to happen."

"These aren't rubies either." He drew his fingers over the wall and the colors of the pattern became brighter. "These are tiles, see?"

"But you're frightened." She took his hand again.

"It was the people in the dream I was afraid of, I'm not scared of Shepp."

"They're watching us."

Randolph was standing in the glow of the fire the boys had built in the room.

"I know," Peter said.

She kissed him.

"They're kissing," Randolph reported.

"Don't care." Shepp's voice sounded far away. "Do what I said."

"Shepp wants to see you, Tot," Randolph called.
She got to her knees. "O.K."

Peter looked at her suspiciously, then felt the bruise on his forehead.

"Does it hurt?"

"I never hit him."

"Oh."

"I will though, wait till he feels it."

"You're too afraid of him to hit him."

"No, I'm not."

"I'd better go now, or else he'll really hurt you. But you should love him anyway, for every hurt he gives you. You can try."

"I was going to tell you," Peter said, looking up at her, "I'm going to hate him to death."

"Oh," she said. She got to her feet, unzipping her jacket. "If you do, it will kill you like weeds covering you up."

"Tell him that," Peter said. "And you have to tell him that you love me. Me!"

"Wait." She went along the wall to the opening and looked in. "Here I am," she said. She pointed her finger. "What are you sitting on?"

Like spirits seated in a cauldron, the boys rested on black stools of which there were three more in the oval-shaped room. The walls were not tiled. One part of the wall had crumbled, showing only darkness behind. The fire was bright, yet there was less smoke than there had been in the tunnel and her eyes didn't sting.

"Well, you don't stand there," said Shepp, "do you? Come in." In the strange light, he looked fat in the face. His eyes and mouth were drained of expression, as though something he had seen had purged him of his thoughts. His forearms rested heavily on his legs, his body pitched forward like a contented man resting in a steam bath.

"All right," she said. She walked over to one of the stools and stared at it, then sat down. The pattern of a jagged tide was in the stone, but it connected a sun with a mountain, a beast she could not identify with a wide-shouldered figure.

"Aren't you going to ask us why I called you?"

"Uh huh," she said. She crushed her hands between her knees.

Shepp wiped his forehead, took off his hat, and set it down by his foot.

"Listen, we figure we're going to be friends with Peter."

She leaned forward now. "You are? You want to be friends with him?"

"No, but we're going to try to, or else he'll get even by blabbing off about everything we found, see?"

"Oh," she said. "Well, that's good."

"He's lucky. But here's something else. We're going to make him pass a test. If he's chicken we don't want him here with us, understand?"

She was silent for a minute, looking from Shepp to Randolph to Chase.

"Don't worry," said Chase. "The test isn't going to hurt him. It's simple. He has to do it though, no matter how stupid he thinks it is, because he has to prove we can trust him." He looked at Shepp for confirmation.

She sat quietly and thought, and when she glanced

up, saw that they were watching her. She took off her jacket. It was better to believe that Shepp meant it, or at least that it would lead to a solution for all of them, than to go on with the fighting.

She sat and thought some more.

"Well?" said Shepp. "Go get him!"

"All right. I guess." She stood up, and avoiding an open pit in the floor, began to leave the room. "Are you sure?"

"Yes. And when you come back, you have to sit by us."

She walked through the entrance and down the tunnel to where Peter sat in front of the low fire.

He wheeled around and looked up at her. "Did you tell him?"

"Tell him what?"

"Don't you remember? What did Shepp say when you told him that you loved me?"

"Oh," she said, "he's not worried about that anymore. He wants to be friends with you."

"Oh!" said Peter, gritting his teeth, his eyes blazing.

"He means it."

"What's the trick?"

"No," she shook her head, still standing, "he means it, Peter."

He inspected her closely. "And you just swallowed it?"

"He's afraid you'll tell everyone about the room and everything."

"Go tell him I won't tell a soul."

"No," she repeated, "this is the chance to be friends with him. He won't pay attention to you anymore; he won't give you any more rules about me. But if you don't see him now, all three of them will jump on you. What will happen then? Please? Stand up. You don't have to do anything he says if you don't want to, just listen to him."

He cradled his face in his hands and stared at the black wind which blew in the underbelly of the fire. There he was, unscrewing the cap of his head, shaking out his brains, and going in to get patted on the back by Shepp because Shepp wanted a favor. It would be nice to watch his enemy back up in his tracks. But Peter knew it would not satisfy him. Still, he said, "I'll listen." He grabbed a piece of wood, stood up, and followed her.

In the oval room sat his enemies. Randolph and Chase held lighted sticks in their hands, and Shepp had taken a place on the floor and was using his throne as a backrest. In the firelight, Randolph's hair was an irritated hue, the color of a red toe.

"Here he is," said Tot. She crossed over the pit and seated herself on one of the stools.

Peter stood in the doorway.

"What?" he said.

"Don't be afraid...."

"I'm not afraid. What do you want?"

Shepp, moving backwards and up, sat on his stool. "Now, look, diddy-doo, you have to be friends - that's what we called you in here for. What are you hiding behind your back?"

"Nothing." Then Peter took a step sideways and his stick came into view.

"Do what we say and you'll be friends with us. Throw the stick on the fire."

"Look at him!" said Randolph. "It's hopeless."

"I'll wait," said Peter.

Shepp stretched out his arm and spread his fingers. "Listen. There's a test. The test is to do what we say. First, get rid of the stick, and then take small steps until you're standing in front of the pit."

Tot sat with her hands pulling down the hair on each side of her face. "This is no way," she said. "Peter, you have to put the stick down."

"It doesn't matter how stupid you think it is," said Chase. "Later on we'll tell you why."

"Do you blame him, though?" Tot asked Shepp.

Then Shepp jumped behind Tot and clasped his hands over her mouth.

"Tot can't talk," he said, "Peter has to talk."

"And she can't say a word until Peter does what we tell him to," said Randolph, "so better drop the stick."

Curses drove in crowds through Peter's head. There would be no bowing, he saw that, unless it was his own to the triple threat of his newly discovered 'friends'. He was furious and humiliated at once as he looked at Tot's mouth covered by Shepp's hand.

"Let her go."

After you, was the meaning of Shepp's nod toward the pit.

Peter dropped the stick and moved into the room until he stood at the edge of the opening.

"Now what?"

"Tell us what it is."

"A well."

"You don't get it," said Shepp. "This is the point." He held Tot's mouth with one hand and poked the finger of his other at the younger boy. "Tot found the tunnel and we discovered the walls and the room. We got the wood and made the fire. But you have to find out something for yourself or else you'll be the only one who didn't help out. You won't care if everyone hears about the place. See?"

"No."

But in Peter's head, his father was showing him the garbage cans in back of the house and a tree flickered. He was supposed to water the tree: it was.

his tree; emptying the garbage made it his house. The truth was, he hadn't made the garbage or the tree. And his father wanted to move. The house would not even be theirs anymore, and the only thing he owned was the jewel inside of him and his freckled skin. But the tunnel was not owned by the boys, if the Indians made it. And it did not belong to the Indians because they were dead. So what was Shepp trying to get at? It was another fable. But here was Peter, bending over the pit as ordered, kicking at the sides and finally lowering himself into it, feeling with his toes the crusted earth which resisted, then broke off and vanished.

Above him, Randolph and Chase watched calmly and Shepp stood behind Tot guarding her mouth.

Then to Peter's eyes, which were about to over-flow, the room spun, and Shepp seemed to slip out of himself like a shadow which slips down a wall. There were two rooms jigging apart. And Shepp was not a person, but the means himself in the working out of Peter's revenge, the ballast dropped from a balloon, a piece of furniture a raging old woman could not tolerate – a color in the mind.

"I know one thing. You couldn't get in here," he told Shepp, "you're too big." Then he hoisted himself out and sat close by.

"O.K., diddy-doo, what is it?"

Peter looked at him. "A fish pond."

Randolph snorted.

Shepp walked over to the hole.

"That hurt," said Tot, moving her tongue around in her mouth and feeling her cheeks.

"I'd have to cut my throat," Shepp frowned at Peter, "before I could find out anything from you."

Shepp turned and lowered himself down. He rested for a moment with his elbows propped on the edges of the hole; then he grunted and kicked his way deeper. Everyone came forward to see.

Suddenly Peter, crabwise, with his feet lifted, scuttled forward and brought both his boots down on Shepp's head. He jumped back.

In the space where Shepp's head had been there was nothing but air now. The hands of Randolph and Chase moved frantically, trying to grab Shepp's clothes. They were reaching for parts of him that were invisible, but the hands kept moving in and out of the hole, as though performing the task unconsciously, like in a dream. After a while, the boys sat up and looked around. Their breath ran in and out, fast. Then they began calling, "Shepp, Shepp," stopping every few seconds to listen.

Tot wailed.

Peter sat across from them – very stiff as though hypnotized, licking his lips. But the others paid no attention to him, as though he were hidden inside a box. Then, when their loss went unredeemed and there was not even a hair of Shepp to prove he had ever existed, Peter became huge in their eyes.

"You'll die," Randolph declared. He stood up, tensed his heavy stomach and clenched his fists.

"I'm going to go too," Tot said suddenly. She put a leg into the hole.

"No you don't," Chase said.

"Yes, I am." Randolph turned for a moment to help Chase and they struggled with her. Her feet pressed against the faces of the boys as they lowered her into the opening. Slowly, they kneeled. It looked as though they were breaking each of her legs.

Her sweater and buttocks and legs disappeared.

Peter lay in an icy calm on the floor. No remorse roared up from his bowels to rack his heart. He lay like an idol-man awaiting a message – in love with freedom from what was to come. Shepp had deserved it – that was Peter's last thought.

Chase sputtered.

Peter lay silently, listening. He pressed his face against the ground as though he could see right through the earth and could see Shepp in the hands of death, and could watch what was happening to him. It was not for Shepp that he worried, but for something inside of himself. He put his eye against the dirt, then rolled his head and scratched his teeth in it – as though live earth touching dead earth could give access to death – listening.

"He can breathe," whispered Peter. He motioned at the hole: wherever Shepp was, there must be air.

Now Randolph and Chase dragged Tot from the

hole – her face swollen with blood. The boys glared at Peter while they held on to her, as though she were the first proof and exhibit of his evil. She struggled and told them to put her down.

"Guard her," said Chase. "We'll make a rope." Bending like a dancer, he began to pull off his trousers while Randolph held Tot in his arms.

A blow fell in the room.

Peter sat up and the others were silent, listening. It came again.

Then Shepp stood in the wall, his jacket, face and trousers dusted with a white chalky substance – his eyes frightened and small as they fixed on Peter. At his feet lay the broken remains of the crumbled wall.

"Ah! Ah!" The two boys at the pit jumped up and rushed screaming at him.

He wiped his mouth and his legs were trembling.

"Shepp," they cried. Then Randolph whirled around and glared at Peter. He pounded his fist in his hand. "We'll kill him now," he said.

But Shepp told him to shut up. Shepp's eyes were

still frightened. He pointed at Peter and said, "You go," - his hands red and swollen.

Peter wiped the perspiration from his face and approached the hole. His stomach rose up in his mouth, he dropped. They watched for him, frozen in their places.

In the darkness, he expected his feet to hit something, but he kept falling. He sank down to his waist in a soft floury stuff. It got into his eyes. It was too dark to see and the burning particles were blinding him. As he struggled in it, he began to tumble forward and down. He reached out with his fingers but there was nothing to hold on to. As he rolled forward, then fell again, he couldn't actually touch anything; it was soft and slow like drifting.

Then he stopped. There was a light; then he realized it could be a color spot in front of his eyes from keeping them pressed shut so tightly against the burning. When he fell over on his back, he knew he had reached bottom and that he was actually seeing.

Looking straight up, he was sure there was a

colored hole. He tried to judge its size. He turned his head from side to side. The light looked like it was coming toward him, then going away again. He didn't know if it was the light that was moving or the darkness that was getting thick and thin around it, or if it was floating or still. First he leaned forward, then his knees straightened as he stood up. But he hit his head against it. he light had never been more than two feet above his head. He knew that if he struck it with a bat, the bat would bounce off.

A voice that came from his stomach said, "Out, get me out of here." His head and his insides hurt. There was stuff stuck in his ears and a scraping noise when he tried to turn around. He began to crawl away from the light and wondered if it would lead him back where he came from. The voice said, "You can do anything you want, just get me out of here." He thought of all the tricks he'd use if he were trying to get away from someone on the street. He promised himself rewards like jewels and a white horse if he could get himself out. But he ended up where he had come from. So he crawled back again past the light and then he came to some fender-like obstructions; large, rough objects. His hands hit against them but it wasn't like hitting a wall. His hands swept, swept along and he followed the walls until he knew he was going up. It was a sort of ramp, but he was circling, because the side he had his hand against kept curving. As he crawled, the place got wider and narrower. He had to flatten out when it got low and then he could smell. Air, without any dust or burning particles in it. He reached up, kept reaching. It was as if the crawling had kept him busy and made him think he had to stay flat when he didn't. He said to himself, "Walk, now, walk." He put out his left hand to touch a wall, and kept moving sideways to his left. Then he moved to his right, then again to his left. It went back and forth. But nothing happened until he went forward with his arms up over his head. His elbows and knees felt the impact. Then he was standing in the room with soft earth and white dust on his arms and all around him. It was as if Shepp, Randolph, Tot, and Chase and the fire and stools had all popped up in a second and they were as surprised as he was. They were staring at him.

Peter's eyes moved slowly around the room.

"What happens, what happens?" Randolph wheezed. His voice sounded distant and faint to Peter.

Shepp nodded. Randolph slowly approached the center of the room, then dropped down the hole. They all waited. He came out in a different place than either Peter or Shepp had. Then Chase dropped down and they waited in a circle for him. Tot went down too, and she appeared from where the wall had already been completely rent.

They stood in a circle then, without saying any-thing.

"I went down," Peter said slowly, "because I kicked Shepp down the hole and he told me to go. When I kicked him, I didn't know what would happen to him. If you want to take revenge on me that's up to you."

"You'll have to do it yourself," Shepp answered. He was still shaking. He looked quickly at Chase and Randolph.

Peter took a seat on the floor. His breath scraped

in his lungs and his head ached. Most of the others too, had felt it. When they came through the wall, the dark stools and the fire and people had all flashed on them as though born in a minute. Except for Shepp. It had been one thing for the others to watch him come through the wall and afterwards go down themselves, but another for Shepp to get kicked in the head and then go through it all without knowing if there was a way out. He had not known himself as he twisted and rolled in the long tumble down. It had made him afraid. And those feelings, even when he had climbed up again and broken through the wall, had not left him.

"What's there to cry about?" "Who cares what happened? No one got killed!"

Randolph nodded at Peter. "That's right. I'm sorry if I was mad at you." He walked over to a stool, sat down and rested his arms on his knees, then put a hand under his shirt and began to scratch as though trying to tear a lump from his belly.

Shepp didn't understand the sudden urge to be apologetic. But he did feel differently toward Peter because it had taken a lot of guts for the younger boy to knock him down the hole. It made Shepp respect him.

"Chase," Tot said dizzily, "aren't you going to pull up your pants?" She had sat down too, fainted for a minute, but no one had noticed. Now she was watching them again.

"We were going to make a rope like with the jackets," Chase explained to Shepp, pulling up his zipper.

"And your pants didn't fall off, crawling around in the dirt?" Shepp asked – his foot tapping up and down like an accordion, while he licked his lips nervously.

"It's my seat." Chase sat up and looked behind him. "I guess my seat's getting big. But that stuff wasn't dirt, look at it. It's more like chalk."

They all laughed, but after a second were quiet again.

"I'm going to sing something," Tot said.

Peter listened. After being frightened in the passageways, he knew he wouldn't be frightened again that day, maybe never. Even if he was trapped by Shepp and the others, or at home, he would be able to think of a way. He owned a head that was filled with all sorts of projects. Some day he would walk up the horizon's arch, find the reasons for things, and help people. He would build buildings, maybe open a store where everyone could try out the stock before they had to pay for it. And at the end of his life, they would put a statue of him in cement in front of the post office. After a while he thought, half aloud, "All those tunnels and curves; they were made!"

"Think they used dynamite?" said Randolph.

"Dynamite!" Shepp's foot was still going. "Dynamite! Didn't you go to school?"

"Same as you," Randolph said. He grinned foolishly at his shoes.

In the soft dust which covered the floor, Peter lay down. He began to draw circles with his finger. At the base of one of the circles he drew a line, then arched forms that resembled birds. Toward the top of the circle, the forms were larger.

Shepp's eyes narrowed. He hopped up and bent

over to look at it. "An emblem? Those are birds and what's that?"

Peter nodded and began to work on another drawing.

"Rocks," Chase said.

"Oh," said Tot, who had left off her singing and came to look. "It's beautiful." Peter glanced up at her and wondered if she was angry at him for knocking Shepp down the hole.

"Make the lower part like the tunnel," said Randolph, moving his fingers in the dirt. "It should be colored like the sand."

"And stars," said Chase. "Five stars, one for each of us."

"An emblem," Randolph announced.

"The birds will be colored white." Bending down, Tot changed the shape of the arched forms with her fingers.

"But who will make them?" Chase asked.

"We can get them made at the bicycle shop," said Shepp. "The guy ordered badges, so he can make some of these."

Peter sat back with his hands propped behind him. "If you were afraid I was going to tell everyone about the tunnel, why should we wear them?" he asked.

"Well of course; what good would they be if we didn't?" asked Shepp. He went back to his stool and sat down.

But it was a little while before anyone said anything.

"You mean everyone will think it's funny and want to know why all of us are wearing them?" asked Tot.

"And," said Randolph, "how are we going to explain how we got to be friends with Peter?"

"We'd have to tell plenty of lies," said Peter, "and tell more to everybody."

"I wouldn't care," said Tot. "I'd put it in a box. I have a lot of things that are too beautiful to wear."

Shepp gnawed his lip. "It doesn't matter about that now," he said. "Later we'll decide. I'll get them made."

"I don't think so," said Peter.

Only a single orange tongue jerked above the pile of blackened wood, and the room was growing dark.

"O.K. Don't worry, diddy-doo. Now the important thing to do is swear. Stand up. Swear that nothing can make us tell what we discovered."

"I don't care if they torture us," said Randolph.

"They can do anything," said Tot. "Never tell."

But Peter was reluctant to swear. "Don't worry, Peter," Tot whispered to him, and her eyes were filled with a kind of urgent bidding, as though she were afraid of her own failure to keep the trust as well as new trouble with Shepp, just when everything was going to be more or less smoothed over. But the sign below Peter of his own making became not as he had intended it, because he was not sure if he had intended it to be anything. He knew Shepp felt differently than he did about the pit and the wall, and somehow, the emblem would be like Shepp's instrument. But he bent his head and extended his hands. All their hands crisscrossed over the emblem, which, because of the dying fire, they could barely see. Eyes closed reverently and lips twitched as they took the oath.

After a few minutes, Shepp noticed his hat and went to pick it up. He began to crunch his heel down on what was left of the fire.

They moved out of the doorway into a darkness which was complete, except for the distant blue spot of light and the red embers of the first fire by the wall. Together they stomped out the coals and walked to the opening and the makeshift rope.

Daylight was shocking.

To them, at least, a day had passed. Yet, by the sun, they could tell it was not far past noon.

How long would they be able to keep their secret?

This is what each of them wondered to himself though no one spoke his thoughts. Instead, alibis were made, and plans for the coming weeks.

By nightfall, Randolph's father, who knew how to get answers to his questions, had learned the whole story.

II

The Indians never saw Shays. They never saw a railroad or a white man. They lived too early and died too quickly to catch a glimpse – as later Indians did – of the people who would transfigure the land – what would grow and prosper, what would die. They decided to plant, even in the barren soil, and became the most peaceful of the tribes. Few men journeyed to their isolated city and the members of the tribe who left to trade with the people to the east and south always returned. The end would come, the old men of the tribe could foresee, when their youths drew on the instincts of the hunt from the people to the north. The northern land provided easy meat, but at the cost of war for the right to it. So their hills became like a vast body with canals and gates, places of storage, drainage and irrigation tunnels – all tiled to prevent the hills from crumbling beneath them. The breath of the city was rain. Rain then was more plentiful. When it did not fall, the city grew still and the old men chose leaders who decided what allotments of food should be given out; then they chewed a bitter cactus plant which for many hours drew them into the sight of the Great Spirit, making their bodies beat with a rhythm that seemed an intimation – if not of rain – at least of future happiness. Their Evil Spirit had brought the dryness, not their God. It would only be to satisfy the earth-killer to spill human or animal blood which – in any event – could not irrigate enough soil to grow even one ear of corn. The Evil Spirit was anything that killed, and the word for evil and the word for killer were synonymous. Violence among the young was not punished, simply ignored. By the time the children reached the age of fourteen years, the need for violence disappeared. If not, youth or man could be banished from the city. But the Indians lived in mistrust of the very land which gave them bread. They named the stars, knew the winds, knew when the rain would fall and also when the drought would set in. But they could imagine a place where drought never was and where their religious enemy did not live. A large poisonous lizard, extinct in the area now but plentiful then, was their embodiment of evil. The lizards were trapped, thrown into a pit and allowed to kill one another. This stinking pit was known as the bowels of the Evil Spirit. It was a strong contrast to the incense and flower-filled room in which every boy and girl at the age of sixteen listened to an Elder recite the origins of the tribe – what manner of men they had come from and what manner they had become. The boy was then given a season in which to decide whether he would stay in the city or leave it. Females were not permitted to choose. If the boy decided to stay, he was introduced to the mysteries and initiated. An explanation of why men had been thrust from a better place they could imagine into the land of death and poison was given by the Elders at this time. A lizard's body was disemboweled and the long intestine dried and treated with gum from a cactus plant. It was then made into an instrument producing a faint echoless music. In the ceremony itself, boys and girls were initiated together and their bodies belonged to the one mind which it was the Indians' purpose to be in constant communion with. Desire was considered to be holy and the rules guiding love were complex. If a man loved a woman, she received him into her house and fed him for two weeks. If after this time she still did not love him, he was forced to leave the city for the same period of time that he had stayed with her; then he had to return and be re-initiated. If a man loved an unmarried woman who was already living with a man, the three of them shared her house for the period of a month. During this time no love-making was permitted unless the lover or the suitor withdrew. After a month's time, if the woman still preferred her lover, the suitor had to leave the city, return, and be re-initiated. Those men and women who lived together for eight seasons and still preferred one another to all suitors could be married.

No suitor could enter their house. A woman was not allowed to enter the house of another woman for purposes of love with a man.

When spells of melancholy came upon the Indians they carved stones with a fitful jagged pattern or made tiles or composed music on their instruments. Melancholy was, in fact, a characteristic of the tribe, as was the saving and transforming of things. Rocks, stones, beans, cornshucks, animal skins, metal - all were transformed or worked into some kind of pattern. But the men felt a sense of their smallness and could not see how it was possible to transform the vast desert into a land of their desire. At the time of their dispersal they had begun to dig wells and troughs in a range of hills sixty miles distant. Their lives never changed. Finally, a great drought, foretold by one of their prophets, brought death and wandering to the entire city. It took only a year for the water and food supplies to run out. Many groups of individuals wandered away, hoping to find water and a place to wait for a few years, before returning. They were either tortured by foreign tribes or initiated into their customs. Most of the Elders stayed on, using the cactus plant to invoke visions of their future home. Old men dropped in the fields, unintentionally delivering into the hands of the earth, the human blood which had been withheld for so long in religious abstinence. For years afterward, troughs and passageways efficiently guided rain water to the fields on the eastern side of the hills. A few wild crops flourished, but no Indians lived to harvest them. Those members of the tribe who returned at a later time had broken their religious pledge not to kill. Their children were swept into the fire of change.

Decades and centuries passed. Tides of sand filled the wells and sealed the openings of the tunnels, and the hills came to look like uninhabited forms again. Buried jewelry, instruments, implements for cooking, rooms with the skulls of the Elders, went unnoticed though men worked just beneath them. Indians who had been moved from their homes in a different state, were hired by a Southerner named Shay for a dollar; they sweated for years without knowing what was ten feet above their heads. They were digging too deep to know and might have preferred not to be told of the battles which proved that such disasters for them were inevitable; their people were being destroyed, the red men did not know how to join together to fight the white men, the commands of great warlike leaders for peace had come too late, and after their people had already been defeated. The most bitter among them could wait through childhood for the Southern nation to defeat the Northern nation, which it did not do; and later, for the German nation to defeat the American and European nations combined, which it did not do. They waited in vain for their land to be returned to them. White men, whose expensive equipment rotted, which in value could clothe and feed all of the tribes and their forefathers as well, the white men, though they practised the same arts of war for which they had condemned the Indians as heathens – still lived and ruled.

*   *   *   *   *   *

The archaeologist gave this information to the assembly at Peter's high school. He was from the State University. Lifting his hands in the darkened auditorium, he pointed to the final slide which showed some workmen and animals standing around the recent excavation.

It was the same gym to which Peter had brought the firemen almost two years before. Into the holes sometimes occupied by badminton standards were thrust tall American flags. A sheet of green plastic was stretched across the ceiling of the gym – a single rent in it permitting a shaft of light to enter the room. The mosaic above the south row of bleachers was dimmed.

The audience wanted to hear more, especially the Indian children; they were hoping the visitor from Tucson would tell about his own experiences in the tunnel. Some of them had been told that the walls in the sacred room could be taken down and built up a hundred times, it wouldn't matter. But the little man put his slides into a box and sat down.

The show, it seemed, was over. The professor

had turned out to be all right. The audience applauded loudly. Then they began to scream. Physical education class was just ten minutes away. If the assembly stretched out for another half hour, they wouldn't have to go out on the field. The bleachers resounded with loud stomps. Open mouths cawed and hallooed. The noise got louder.

Mrs. Bright, the superintendent, stood at the microphone in the center of the echoes. "If you don't quiet down," she said, "the assembly will be dismissed ... this minute ... there will be no presentation by the three boys who are waiting to speak."

In about five seconds the room was still.

Mrs. Bright knew that a couple of other students had taken part in the discovery too, but she had gone through with the program on the condition that the account of the adventure would make no mention of them. There had been enough trouble already that term. Four months earlier she had conducted a pregnant girl home from school. About six weeks after that, a boy was killed on the road three miles outside of town. These two events and the alarm which had accompanied them had been like twisting serpents held at arm's length from her exposed body. But she had managed to control the situation. The girl and her mother were planning to leave Shays that very day. The parents of the dead boy had promised to build a memorial row of benches around the flagpole area of the school. The three students who remained of the original five discoverers of the tunnel had agreed to tell what had happened to each of them individually without getting into a discussion of the recent troubles in front of the assembly.

Shepp, Randolph and Chase sat at the table to her left, glancing up at the superintendent and at each other as though getting ready to surprise the audience and maybe themselves. They were wearing stiff white shirts and suits which - from the upper galleries - looked like cardboard cutouts. The neck on Chase's shirt was too small for him but instead of unfastening it, he was satisfied to loosen the knot of his tie.

The vacancy into which they had all been reaching was not the pit in the floor down which Peter had kicked Shepp, but the disappearance of Peter himself – something they still struggled with and tried to comprehend.

Why wouldn't the superintendent allow them to talk about Peter in front of everyone? Did he frighten her more than the story of the tunnel itself? She had seemed to admire them when they told her what happened. She had heard it twice already – each time encouraging them, groaning and shaking her head, saying it was difficult to believe that such a thing had actually taken place. How could they get through it without serious injury? She knew she would have cried and become so scared she wouldn't have been able to move once she was in the passage-ways under the floor. She did admire them. The capacities of chidren amazed and frightened her.

Shepp was supposed to speak first. He had driven to the tunnel with Peter a second time – before a cord had been unwound beneath the surface of the hills. Peter had proved the wild story he had told Shepp, that the oval room was still being used. But no one in the whole auditorium could understand the troubles Shepp had now. Tot was going to have a baby. He

wasn't even sure it was his. Also, Shepp had been
given the key to the school athletic locker and had
been put in charge of the equipment. Recently, he
had been accused of a theft amounting to more than a
hundred dollars. He wanted to go into the army as
soon as possible. A few years in a distant country
would be a good way to relax. Any more trouble
would get him expelled from the school.

All three boys thought that Peter's death made
his part in the discovery even more important. In
the name - not of a mouldering body, the parts of
which had not been buried intact - but of a spirit
of coherence and unity, they had decided to tell how
Peter had caused them all to drop down into the hole.

The details of Peter's death no one knew. A story
had gone around telling of several all-night meetings
between Tot and Peter arranged in the tunnel under
the very noses of the archeologists. An early morning return trip from one of these meetings turned
out to be fatal. Peter was flung toward the stars by
a speeding Greyhound bus and Tot - afraid of being
discovered (at the time she must have known she

was pregnant) escaped into the darkness and returned to school only for a day - then disappeared
again. No one had gone to see her - secluded as she
was in the heavenly lights and mysterious processes
of maternity. But Shepp had never believed the story
and had convinced Randolph, Chase, and several
others not to believe it either. He knew that on the
quiet, an investigation was in progress. Someone
high up in city government, who was angry with the
highway department, claimed that it was another
example of the carelessness of the large transpor-
tation companies. There was a human body for sure,
but one that no reporter was going to photograph for
the morning newspapers. Only the boy's parents had
been allowed to see it. They were especially upset
because the identification of the boy could never be
complete. This led to the belief, which Shepp went
along with - that Peter could still be alive. There
was a vacancy - an absence - where the primary
means of identification is usually found. For some
reason the city officials and local police were out-
raged. It had been as though the road which led

east went only a little way now, the rest of the distance being occupied by an ocean or waterfalls. Everyone had wanted to talk about it, but no one knew how. The odd coat, the torso and legs, were, however, identified by the parents as belonging to their son. In any case, the three boys did not think it was Peter who had gotten Tot pregnant, even though the superintendent might see a connection.

She smiled at the boys then spoke to the hundreds of faces in the bleachers.

"The boys who first discovered the Indian ruins are going to tell you what happened to them ... and what it was like to find the tunnel without knowing any of the things which Dr. Blicks has presented. Other people would have been more cautious than they were - and perhaps they should have worried seriously about the dangers involved. But the boys will tell you their experiences for themselves."

While she was talking, Shepp leaned over and told Chase to go first. Chase's lower jaw was like a bald purse that didn't want to open unless it had to. A second later, Shepp promised him a pair of auto tires. Chase didn't have a car yet, but he nodded.

"Shepp, will you tell us what happened the day you went into the desert in the direction of the mines?"

"I'm going to talk first," Chase said. He glanced at her quickly. Her knees were bent – she was about to sit down in her chair – then she shook her head at him.

The back of his chair tipped forward as he lowered his head down to the microphone.

She opened her mouth very wide and tapped the side of her cheek.

"The room in the slides," he began, his voice very low, "had the stools in a circle ... it was like a ring. Only the walls weren't all broken like they are in the picture ... no ... we tried to figure out what the pit in the floor was used for. Shepp got into it ... up to his shoulders ... just when he was feeling the inside with his feet, Peter Poole jumped forward ... Peter had followed us out there ... he was mad at Shepp ... and he jumped on Shepp's head and knocked him out of sight ..."

There was a complete silence as though the room had disappeared along with the head Peter had kicked ... then there were shrieks, applause, and laughter.

When Chase looked up, Mrs. Bright smiled at him. Not her usual smile. Inside the teeth, there seemed to be a different emotion for which she hadn't found an expression yet.

She stood up and shifted her weight from foot to foot. There was no controlling the boys once they had decided to do something. They had planned to trick her and would probably carry the thing too far unless she managed to stop it.

She stood at the microphone again. "But you didn't go into the hole first, that's why I asked Shepp to speak first. And you disobeyed me." A chilly silence followed this announcement. Her attention was drawn to his shoulders. A kind of restless shifting and strain beneath his jacket, a movement there gave her the impression he was changing or transforming. She might have been watching something in the distance struggling up in feathery movements from the floor.

"Shepp?" she said.

But the dark-haired boy gestured to Chase, signifying that he could tell it better.

Looking hard at the clock she brought her palms together twice. The claps were loud.

"We will have to stop here, we are very close to the bell. Perhaps we should show our appreciation to Dr. Blicks again, after which we will be dismissed."

Raising her hands again, she tried to lead the applause but all she heard were groans.

Chase sat at the table as though wondering how he could change some of the things he had said – as though he had been talking in his sleep without being aware of it. The other two boys were whispering to each other, trying to guess what would happen to them.

Dr. Blicks left his chair and approached the superintendent.

"I am so sorry," he whispered. "This is not the end, is it? They were in the room where the initiations took place. After about a thousand years, they went through ceremonies exactly the same as the Indians. May I talk to them about it ... in your office ... or in an empty classroom?"

Mrs. Bright's hand closed on his shoulder and she whispered in his ear. "In my office will be fine."

The audience saw the professor sit down.

"Now, applause is in order for Dr. Blicks. Let's show our appreciation.

This time, a roar answered her appeal, and the students jumped over the bleachers and departed in noisy groups.

The professor hurried around the edge of the table and followed the superintendent.

"I apologize," she said.

"The boys will probably exaggerate a little, but that's all right. It's important. I love to hear them, that's why I came today."

"I love children too." At that moment, however, she thought the best way to show her love would be to quit her job and give it to someone with inspiration. Mrs. Bright signalled them, and the boys followed the tall curly-haired woman and the balding professor out of the gym and along a covered pathway.

"There's a lot more stuff to tell," Randolph said, popping his fingers and smacking his fist into his palm. "I can tell about the emblem Peter drew."

Chase gave a warning about being kicked out, then squeezed the back of Randolph's neck.

"I sure will," Randolph added, "I'll tell every word he said."

Shepp sauntered ahead of them. They jolted with short steps behind the tall boy, but didn't seem to make much progress up the walk. Shepp waited by the door of Mrs. Bright's office until they caught up.

"Tomorrow, you'll see those tires."

Chase grunted and gave a nod.

Mrs. Bright opened the blinds a little. The sun was around the other side of the building.

While the boys and the professor got seated, a thought gained control of her mind again and made itself clear at last – something that had been bothering her from the first minute she had seen the professor out in the parking lot. Though he had a bald patch on top of his head, a varnished nut-color from the sun - he was almost a perfect double for Mrs. Bright's mother. The superintendent had a quirk: often, she could see people as either male or female. Mentally, she pictured fluffed-out blonde curls around Dr. Blicks until feature by feature he was transformed into a double of the dead mother. It was like having the old woman nearby again. Mrs. Bright had loved her father too, worshipped him, until recently. The change had given her a cynical attitude toward other people's certainties. All the time she had loved him and trusted him, she had been unaware of the truth. People might think they were sure of what they loved and hated, but time could change the deepest faith. She had not exactly become self-destructive, but she wondered why she had a position of responsibility. Her life was shallow. Everyone around her was shallow. Yet every day she told the children that they must become worthy of Shays and their country. If everyone knew how ugly the taste of self-doubt could be, they wouldn't be rushing around expecting other people to tell them what to do. Trust. The weakest and saddest of all impulses. Her younger brother – six years her junior – had become a political liberal as he matured. He was in his late thirties now and didn't obey the rules of decorum about his older sister the way he used to. One evening he described the fact that their perfect father had been seeing women all the time that they were growing up. A man who had pretended to be the source of morality and inspiration to the other members of the family. No doubt, most of the actualities of the world were like that. She hadn't spoken to her brother since, but she believed him.

It made her feel good now, to have the professor there, a helpful, agreeable person, a double for someone who had been reliable until the day she died. The boys might want to defy their superintendent, but Dr. Blicks could ask them all the questions he wanted to, until he was satisfied. It could take the whole afternoon, if necessary.

"Are you ready, Doctor?" She smiled and stroked the arm of her chair.

"Yes. Thank you. We will begin again. I'm intensely interested in what you have to say, Chase, so don't leave out a single detail."

The pain which Chase had seen behind the superintendent's smile was gone now. He glanced at her once more to make sure - before speaking.

He described the struggle they had had with Peter at the tunnel and how they had devised a test for him in the oval room. "But it backfired, and Shepp got kicked down the hole before we could do anything about it. Then, when he came through the wall, Peter went next, then Randolph, and I was fourth. Randolph said I should go and Shepp agreed. I wanted to go anyway, so I jumped in. But there was no bottom. My feet never hit anything. All of a sudden, I was in this soft powdery stuff. It burned my eyes. I just hoped it would disappear -"

"Good!" said the archeologist. "Where is Peter? Is he here?" He flapped open his tweed jacket and shifted in his chair as though looking for Peter somewhere behind him.

"Peter was killed not long ago," said Mrs.

Bright, still smiling.

"Ah!" Dr. Blicks murmured, "how?"

She leaned across the desk and her mouth wrinkled before she spoke. "An accident in a dust storm. They say he was hit by a bus."

Peter had been so odd that she had always known something unpredictable would happen to him.

The superintendent motioned for Chase to continue.

"Yes, Ma'am." The boy went on to describe what it was like to crawl in the twisting passageways beneath the earth. Finally he came to the end of his narrative. "That was it."

"Except," Randolph sang out, "later, Peter Poole drew an emblem. He drew it on the floor of the room."

"Thank you," said the archeologist. "I can feel it. A suffocating experience, full of discomfort and darkness. Then suddenly, you come out."

He sat forward, elbows on knees, took off his glasses and rubbed the skin on his forehead.

"Now, are there any other questions you would

like to ask?" Mrs. Bright leaned forward too, and waited for his answer.

"Well, I might as well tell you," he said to the superintendent, "the first substance, the powdery stuff the boys jumped into –that stings the eyes – are ashes of the dead Indians."

Her hand disappeared into her mouth, then she brought both fists down on the desk. She shook her head at him.

The archeologist nodded.

"It should be fogotten then," she declared. Her fingers seemed to be begging him to return to a sensible manner of speaking. "It should be kept a secret," she repeated.

"But you see how Chase –"

"Covered from head to toe with, and smothered with ashes of dead Indians!" Mrs. Bright said half to the boys, half to herself, and stared at them as though they were ghosts.

The faces of the three boys were contorted with the news. Randolph's especially. His tongue hung out of his teeth like that of a man who has been strangled.

Chase felt his cheeks with one hand and pulled at his shirt with the other. The expression of a fish - sucked-in cheeks, swollen lips - showed that Shepp was disgusted.

"Oh well, it's not so bad," Dr. Blicks told them, "until you find out .... They were just ashes."

"But, Doctor, I'm sorry," said Mrs. Bright, slowly getting to her feet, "I strongly feel that -"

"What? That I'm just indulging myself to enjoy a funny joke? No, I don't enjoy it."

With these words, Mrs. Bright fell back into her chair.

Following a brief knock, the door swung open and an unexpected visitor - an unwelcome one, judging from the reactions - whose dress was so long it flowed around her like water, entered the room and stood for a moment while all eyes fastened on her midriff, which was heaving with the effort of her journey from the parking lot.

Tot didn't expect a noisy welcome, but the frowns of Mrs. Bright and Shepp were discouraging. She smiled at everyone before she moved to a chair next to Shepp. She was carrying a large folder pressed against her stomach.

Shepp moved his chair away from her and then watched her carefully.

She had been led on her mission by a sound which ears that want to hear in the darkness know – all the trouble and hurt which grow with uncertainty. It was probably the last time she would see her friends. A part of her life was going to end soon. Where she and her mother were going, no one would recognize her – no one would have ever seen Peter.

Mrs. Bright had shown on several occasions that she was not fond of Tot. She had reasons, but couldn't define them. Over the phone, several weeks before, she had surprised herself by saying to Tot's mother, "Yes, I'm afraid it's true, I don't like her." Mrs. Bright's secretary had glanced up with a puzzled expression. The way Mrs. Bright saw it, she and Tot were at opposite ends of a teeter-totter, moving between the depths of evil and the bosom of heaven. Tot too often seemed to be completely at ease. In a town as lacking in inspiration as Shays, so full of malfunction and weakness, no one deserved to see herself as asleep in paradise like Tot did - asleep in the lap of God after a good deal of premature sex.

"You have interrupted us. And ... I'm distressed to see you." Mrs. Bright pointed at her with a stiff finger. "What's the idea?"

"Right! What are you doing here?" Shepp whispered.

"Hush," she told him. She crossed her arms on the folder.

"I said, what are you doing here?" He was afraid she had come to make him pay the price.

"I'm sorry I'm late," she said softly, "but it's only right I should be here. I was the one who found the tunnel."

She looked at Chase for confirmation. He nodded and bumped Randolph.

Immediately upon Tot's entrance, the archeologist had asked Randolph, "Who is she?" Now he said, "You? You were the one who found the tunnel? Not the other boy, Peter?"

"Yes," she replied.

Dr. Blicks laughed, then pushed his face into his hands.

"What's the difference," asked Mrs. Bright. "The point is, what do you want?"

"I came to read something that Peter wrote." Tot knew she had hurt Peter's feelings one time by not paying enough attention to the pages that were in the folder. She unclasped the flap and took them out. Somehow, she felt implicated in Peter's death; she could not understand it.

"It doesn't matter so much about my part in the discovery," Tot said. "But I have to read this story."

"But you can't today," said Mrs. Bright.

"It's important."

"I don't care." The superintendent's fingers rose upward. When they withdrew from her hair, one section was wild and kinky. "Let me tell you something, Tot. Dr. Blicks has informed us of a few things concerning the passageway that you had no way of knowing. We're all upset now. The whole trouble you've gone to and the story too, whatever it might be, would definitely be too much."

"Then this will make you feel better. There's no way that Peter can come back. That's why the story should be heard."

"Perhaps another time," said Mrs. Bright. "Please! Let's do it another time. The Doctor is asking the boys questions. If you must intrude ... honestly, I would prefer that you go, or that we all go. Isn't your mother waiting for you outside?"

Tot reached for the papers. But the archeologist had already motioned for Shepp to pass them down and now the Doctor was studying them.

Mrs. Bright glanced at Dr. Blicks, then back at Tot. She licked her lips and tapped her fingers on the desk.

"You will find, now that you have suddenly become older, it is not an easy thing to be good, it isn't an easy thing. We have to get over the idea that because we want something, it's good, because it appears to be pleasant, because we're attached to it. Now, as for Peter, I can agree with you about one thing only, that he often showed himself to be unlike anyone else on earth.

"But the way you say this isn't right," Tot replied.

"Your friends wouldn't deny it. There's the matter of his pajamas. Randolph?"

Randolph nodded at her and licked his lips. The freckles on Randolph's lips had automatically made half of the females in the school uninterested in him as a possible boyfriend. It had become increasingly hard for him to think of himself as the double of Chase. Chase had gotten wide in the shoulders and put on weight and the girls were phoning him up at night and taking up his time. Randolph went around smacking his fist into his palm, hoping to see a good fight. Now his eyes snapped with a kind of deliberate malice.

"Why did Peter put his pants on over his pajamas? Why did he wear pajamas to school all the time, Randolph?"

"Don't ask me, Mrs. Bright," he answered. "But I guess he had a good reason."

"That's what I wonder about myself." Mrs. Bright thanked him and clicked her teeth. She turned to Chase and asked him the same question. He turned his head from side to side as though he were trying to avoid the jabs of a stick.

"They don't know anything about it," Tot said.

"Maybe if he started staring at this place and thought about it for thirty minutes, it might turn into something else like a toad or a garage," Shepp offered. "Maybe it wouldn't be here anymore."

"That was exactly my point," said the superintendent.

"What a lie!" Tot cried. "If Shepp hadn't hit Peter so many times, he wouldn't have gotten kicked down the hole. That's what made him afraid, Shepp had to go first, and that's the truth."

When Shepp turned to her, his face was blank - which was the expression he usually wore before he pounded someone. It was a lot of back talk for Shepp to swallow. She wan't easy to understand. In every respect she seemed a different girl from the one who had walked with him to the mines two years before. No lines deepened her face, but her eyes had a light in them like a wild animal. He wished Peter were alive. If he were there, maybe the blame could be pinned on him.

"You show a lot of enthusiasm for your lost companion," the archeologist observed, tapping the pages on the desk. "And what a wonderful way of saying things you have." He set the pages on the tabletop.

"The writing is not important to us, but I must admit, extremely interesting. You know, the information I have given you inside the auditorium is eclectic, and not complete. That is, I and my colleagues, have assumed that the Indians who constructed the tunnel were similar to other tribes who lived in the area and originally even borrowed some customs and beliefs from them. However, the hills are just opened to us for a short time. We should be able to find out much more in the future. But from Chase's account before, I understand there must have been some trouble between you children at first, yes?"

"Yes, there was," said Tot.

"And the chamber, though terrifying, was of benefit; but the effects of such an experience don't last long."

"No?" Tot said. "The tunnel kept some of us interested for a pretty long time."

Mrs. Bright shot a glance at Tot before crossing her arms on her breast. "From the girl's viewpoint, she might be right. But I have a question to ask that is going to sound silly, because it is so basic and no one has brought it up yet. To you it might sound like a frightened woman talking. But what if the passage-way had been a maze and Shepp had suffocated or broken his neck in it?"

The Doctor ruffled the fringe of hair above his ears and shrugged.

"You don't care?" Mrs. Bright moved closer to the desk, her face showing disbelief. "You see, Doctor, they were all frightened by the experience, but this boy more so. Isn't that true, Shepp? You told me once that you didn't think the hole was such a good thing?"

Shepp smiled and screwed his thumbs into his eyes before nodding at Mrs. Bright. "That's right."

"Oh," said Tot. "I already told you why."

"Forget it!" Shepp laughed, then gave her a challenging stare. She thought she could talk to him any way she wanted to. She had something on him, it was true. But she was the one who had stopped seeing him, saying it wasn't going right anymore. He could take her or leave her.

"That's the truth. I just don't think it was a good idea, Mrs. Bright." He swiveled his head on his thumbs again, then added, "There was just nothing to it."

"Chase gave us a picture of many exciting events."

"O.K." The corner of his mouth opened wide. He leaned against the desk and pointed a finger as though sighting a target. "Let me figure .... What would be the difference if I had a hundred and thirty pound ball like a lead basketball, or Randolph, who weighs about the same thing? If I drop them at the same time, what happens? I don't get excited about feeling like a piece of athletic equipment. It topples over, it bounces off a wall. What can I do about it? Maybe that's the ticket for some people, but not me."

Randolph laughed.

Mrs. Bright nodded quickly. "Finding yourself in a situation which is so disagreeable and uncomfortable and not understanding it –"

"And I'll tell you another thing," Shepp said. "It didn't destroy me."

The two other boys – and even Tot – laughed then. The idea of anything destroying Shepp was funny. He had, in fact, destroyed the Chinese terror from Silverton not three months before. The Chinaman who had, until then, been the Sphinx of the desert.

Then Tot stopped laughing and she wanted to cry. "That's because you won't let yourself feel how important it is, or how important Peter was, or I am," she said. "Yes, for instance, how important I am."

Dr. Blicks set both feet squarely on the floor and rubbed his hands together. "This is silly. Whether or not the boy can understand what happened to the others or the value of the initiation for the Indians is beside the point."

"No, Doctor," Mrs. Bright said, trying to smile. "I had no way of knowing what he was going to say –"

Then she laughed. Everyone was laughing. The laughter seemed to sing out as though from little sculptured mouths in the walls of the room.

"No insult intended, Doctor. If I had known you were going to become angry –" The superintendent flexed her hands and shook her head, still smiling.

"Didn't anyone tell you about the emblem?" Tot asked.

"The emblem that Peter drew on the floor of the room after we came out of the walls," Randolph murmured.

"One of the boys mentioned it, yes," the archeologist said.

"Thank you." Mrs. Bright nodded at Randolph. Then she passed her hand over her eyes. Once again, she felt inadequate, in need of exciting ideas. Someone inspired should be there. She sighed. "Well, perhaps it's futile to talk about something that's past."

"But it isn't past," Tot said. She stood up. "If you aren't going to read that book now, "I'll send everyone a copy as soon as I can make them. But you can keep this copy, Mrs. Bright. It's Peter's book about life. Maybe he wouldn't have been able to write it if we hadn't gone out to the tunnel, or done anything except want to blow everyone up."

She looked at Chase and Randolph. "Good-bye," she said. Then she maneuvered sideways past Shepp and opened the door.

After the door closed, the superintendent stood up. "Do you boys want to leave now?"

They looked at each other, then filed out, nodding at Mrs. Bright and the archeologist.

"Thank you, boys," Dr. Blicks said. "Especially my thanks to you, Chase."

Outside, they ran after Tot. She was at the edge of the parking lot when they caught up with her, walking in the direction of her mother's car.

"Wow, look at that," Chase said. Across the street was Tot's house, tilted slightly and festooned as though it had been torn by force from its foundations; the building rested on the long body of a moving truck. Metal devices supported it from behind. The eaves, it seemed, would knock over the streetlamps.

"I didn't know you were taking your house too," Chase exclaimed.

She looked at it, then began to tighten the clip in her hair. It was good to stand for a minute with nothing more to say while the clouds moved in a slow chain into the east.

"Old bitch Bright was mad in the gym," Randolph snorted, "but I don't think she's going to do anything to us."

Chase shook his head. "I'm glad to be out of there."

Already, Tot was thinking of the journey and the rolling hills where she was going.

Then she looked at Shepp. "I'm mad at you."

He had taken off his jacket, and was unsliding his tie.

"It's not my fault, is it? What did I do?"

"You could have called me. It's been much too easy for you. You could at least have called me."

"You mean, give in: take care of you and your mother; feed your baby too for the rest of my life . . . ."

"My mother's taking me out of here without needing any help from you. The baby had better be Peter's, Shepp. If it isn't, I'll put it in a box of oranges and set it on the railroad track. Then it will be an eye for an eye."

He stared at her, scratching his head. Then he said, "I don't believe you."

In her long dress and with her body like one shape sleeping in the other, she walked to the waiting car and got in. She really didn't know whose it was. She thought of herself as stupid though not long ago someone had thought she was more than that.

"Do you think she means it?" Randolph asked.

"Naw ... you idiot. Christ! That one is too hot for me! Look at her. Just taking off!"

The boys watched the car disappear, then sauntered out to the street to study the house. When it began to move, it resembled a ship sailing along the avenue.

Mrs. Bright and the archeologist were still talking in her office, about to shake hands. The superintendent's hands were wet.

"I hope everything went the way you wanted it to, Doctor. I'd feel terrible if you were upset. We had rude interruptions. If only people weren't so rude."

"On the contrary. It helped."

She gulped and picked a small burr from the sleeve of her dress, wondering how it had escaped her notice.

"Do you remember," she went on, "that I mentioned a consideration that we are going to send you? It won't be much. . ."

The archeologist shook his head rapidly. "No, no, no, no."

He opened the door. "The parking lot is just through the side entrance and to the left?"

She nodded. "Goodbye!" Her hands clutched his, then she watched him go. After he was out of sight, she stepped back into the room, drew the blinds and sat down for more than an hour – as motionless in her chair as though paralyzed by an electrical current.

Surveying the room when she stood up again, she

felt almost as though she had returned from the grave
and had no crucial interests in her office.

"What do I need, what do I need?" She scratched
her scalp furiously. Something had to fill up the time
before she went back to her paperwork at home. Then
she remembered. A steak house – a franchise from
California – had opened, a new place that people said
was unique. She hadn't tried it yet. Instead of going
home for dinner, she'd give herself a treat.

III

It took Peter four weeks to find the materials for the work. Then he decided it had to be much bigger, the size of an actual head. He travelled to washes where sudden floods ranged down from the high mountains that were barely visible from the town of Shays. He found beautiful crystals there. On hands and knees, he crept through channeled gullies; dust that was hot like silk, was strained through his fingers while he looked for bits of black metal. Wherever rocks made a protective shelf, he searched for beetle-shaped stones and wood hardened to glass. He hunted in the city too. Surrounded in the park by citizens who knew how but not what, he crept into clumps of brush beneath the cottonwoods and juniper, searching the earth. There indeed he found what he wanted, especially some tiny snail shells that would be perfect for eyes. Hard too.

Then the work began. In the shop at school, later at home in his closet – it took more time than he had expected. He used a board for the base and good stiff wire for the shape. By the time he was finished, a month had passed. Already children had gone up to the mountains, to the sacred woods in the fall sun.

The work wasn't to bribe Tot. It wasn't of him. Not like photographs passed around in school, either. He didn't want to just give it to her as he had first planned, but thought he should take her some place and dance with her before she saw it. He thought of the tunnel. But there wasn't any way to carry it out there. So he told her to meet him by the escape hatch which led out from his room. His parents had been trying to keep him from leaving the house in the middle of the night, and had put a lock on his door and fastened the screen of his window from the outside. One day soon, they promised, he was going to be sent away to school.

"Come in, quick."

He lifted up the earth-covered board all the way. Soon they stood inside his room. He picked up his flashlight and turned it on the sculpture where it leaned from the top of the dresser against the wall.

No matter how close he pressed his lips to her ear, he wanted to stand right inside of her so that when he thought things, she could hear them.

Now he had to say, "Shhh," and jab his thumb at the wall. "My mother is right ... in ... there."

In the likeness, Tot's cheeks, in layers of stone, were puffed as though with the desert wind, and her lips were open. The sculpture looked like a shouting girl, full of a happiness that was invisible to her always, that came without stopping from the feelings inside her.

For a minute, seeing Tot's smile, Peter didn't care if he had plenty to do. He didn't want to leave the room now. It was as though the making of the sculpture had taught him some secret knowledge about her.

"Can I look at it some more?" she asked.

Peter told her to get into his bed and shine the

flashlight on the sculpture and look at it all night if she wanted to. He was going out to the tunnel. She had to keep watch for him in case his mother returned to his room to make a check. If Tot heard the lock. she was to turn off his flashlight and cover herself up. Peter felt her arm. "Make your arm stiff," he said, "make everything hard so that you'll feel more like me." He gave her some pajama tops. "Let these stick out and she won't know what part she's feeling." He unscrewed the bulb in the lamp so if his mother tried to turn on the light she wouldn't be able to see. Then he was gone.

Tot didn't say no or yes. She had never anticipated spending the night in bed for Peter while he made a trip to the tunnel. The portrait in stones, though, spoke many words for him. Peter was devoted and yet demanding. Shepp, in his own way, expected less of her. With him, she went places that Peter would never think of taking her. For instance, whenever Shepp could get his black vehicle working, he took her out to a drive-in restaurant where he would either watch fights or get into them. One night, Tot lost her way among a maze of car bumpers and fenders, trying to find the ladies' room. She had knocked into an open car door. Stunned, she saw in the back seat three people crowded together like large birds - a naked figure sighing beneath them. And soaring out toward Tot from the back seat were the girl's pinioned legs. Tot had run away and wanted to escape from the place and never go back again. Would she, though, go back, the next time Shepp came by for her? At that time, she didn't know. The whole thing was becoming hopeless.

But looking at the face to which the flashlight gave a solitary life, she decided that only a person who could think of her that way really loved her. What could she do for Peter? He was troubling himself with things that didn't have to be so much trouble. She was certain of it. She would have to talk to him about the bad opinion he had of himself. After about an hour - though she knew he wanted her to keep watch for him - she left the bed. Wrapping a blanket around her shoulders, she crawled out of the escape hatch and set off in the direction of the tunnel, hurrying away from the moon.

Peter, meanwhile, was staring at a light which was like a smoky coal flame; it was coming from the direction of the oval room. Filtering along the walls and openings in the hillsides came sounds that made him hold his breath, trying to identify them. A wind seemed to be dissolving them as soon as they were uttered. But no wind had blown along the highway or through the sage. His hands relaxed, tightened again on the iron rungs of the ladder. Looking behind him he descended another step. He knew, from the noises, that it was not the other boys who had come out to make plans. Perhaps it was the intervening earth itself which gave the sounds the sense of being born and drowned in the same moment.

Finally, his feet touched the floor of the tunnel. Led by the light, he crept forward. The sounds grew in volume but were no more distinct.

Were these voices that could not rest, ghosts of the dead Indians, come back to repeat their songs? If so, breath by breath, their knotted history released its pain in night music that no one would ever hear unless they came to listen in the solitude of the tunnel. It was like a timeless voice built into the place for the benefit of the makers of the colored walls and simple jewelry.

Peter came to a stop where the water channels fed into the main passageway. To his left, he could see in a distant chamber the source of the sounds. He felt as though he were looking from the earth into a different world. He put out his hand, not to stop it, but wanting to touch what he saw. The sounds he had heard were human, but if the authors were ghosts, they were not tired of their bodies, but had returned in the forms in which the Great Spirit had once made them. Men naked to the waist passed to and fro in an atmosphere that looked like it was filled with soot. Music, voices that were mixed in a feeble chant struggled, then mingled with the crusts of the earth's underbody.

Suddenly, the men were silent. They sat down, their arms linked. Then they hummed a single note into each other's bones. The Indian in the center rose with his knees close together. A wave motion travelled through his ankles, up through his hips to his shoulders and head, ending with the final downward motion of his body as he dropped into the hole and disappeared. At first, the other men didn't seem to realize he was gone. They froze in their places with their eyes fixed on the opening. Then they snapped their fingers in each other's faces. Another man came to the center. He rolled his head in a circle and his tongue stuck out of his mouth. He opened his eyes wide as possible; slowly his right hand reached around and grabbed the hair on the back of his head and pulled downward; his chin tilted upward and his tongue remained outstretched. What were the other Indians saying to him? From their tones, it seemed to be a mixture of accusations and apologies. The man nodded, still holding on to his head in the strange way. Whack! One of the stools was used as a drum. The sound was like a gunshot. Suddenly, the man rose to his feet. The wave motion passed through his body and he dropped down the hole. Another man rose. The impulse went through his body, then he leaped in jerky motions around the seated Indians before pitching himself head first into the opening at their feet. Then the largest of them moved into the center of the circle. He gathered the heads of two others against his chest and rolled them gently against his skin, but the men across from him made him let go. Tears filled his eyes. He bared his teeth, then guided himself an inch at a time to the central opening. The flame of the fire in the room was like a thick coal flame that dragged its way along the piled earth. The large man went down slowly, like the tongue of the flame. Finally, only three men were left; they lay flat on the floor as though dead. With the simultaneous tone of a loud note hummed by the men and the walls themselves, the boundaries of the room fell in seven sections; the Indians who had vanished, now covered with white ashes, entered the room again. They took hands.

Peter stepped back. His own voice, would they hear him if he shouted? But he was afraid to do that. Though emotion jetted from the walls, he was silent, not wanting to be discovered, not wanting them to hear him. With a burning sensation in the top of his skull, he backed without a sound, down the length of the tunnel. Then once more he was on the surface. He ran up the slope in the night and lay down on a rock. From where he rested, catching his breath, he could see the location of the tunnel and the approach to it.

After a while, a small figure appeared, wrapped-up and moving slowly, bird-like, along the incline, in the direction of the hole.

Peter studied the form. Then he rushed down the slope.

"This way. Tot!"

A belt of pointed stars had just come up over the mountain. In the other direction, the moon had already set, but the stars were nearly bright enough to cast a shadow.

Tot was tired from her walk. She sat down on the rock and rested, breathing hard. He kept his eyes fastened on the hole.

"They're making the earth in there," he murmured. He pointed down. "The Indians. There are Indians in the room. I just saw them."

"What are they doing?"

After he described what he had seen, she realized that the men were going to come out again.

"They must be from the reservation," she said. A small band, of about four hundred members, the descendants of Indians from a different part of the state, lived on a few hundred acres south of town. Supposedly, there was a canyon with a stream and some immense trees there.

"Did they see you?"

"No." He pressed her arm. "We have to wait." But Peter wasn't certain that the men he had seen were real, could live anywhere but in the oval room, could come out of the hole into the night.

"Do you really think that's what they're doing, making the world, Peter?"

"This is the way the earth was made. There was a flood. They hid in the hills and they made a plan, what to do when the water went down again."

Tot leaned against him. Strands of her hair caught in his eyelashes and curled around his ears; she pressed against his side.

She had followed him because she wanted to be near him. Although she complained about the cold, her hands were hot on his neck and her breath warmed him. He relaxed, her mouth pressed against his neck, and then, there were gaping holes in his shirt and beneath his belt. Her fingers there were like the tails of little creatures from a tropic lake. It was flying out there.

She caught him. He pressed his mouth against her hair. It was flying out there. She caught him and he bumped against her. Then she drew him into the strange smell of her body. As though he were able to swim, he wandered along the walls of the inner room, aloft on her strong belly while she did his motion in opposite in swimming motions below.

From stomach to neck he quivered. It was hard to know if they were still in the blanket or hanging over the edge of the earth, floating free among the stars, free to dwell in many worlds and to visit many. People said men had once lived on a different planet. As he watched the brightest star turn from red to green to blue, he knew that someday he would find out.

He felt Tot smiling against his ear. Then he stood up on the rock. She guided his hand to her lips.

Now he felt like one person who had never known until now that he had been separated into two.

"Have you ever done that with Shepp?"

She didn't answer. He kept asking her and finally she told him. But when she wanted to know if he minded, he was silent. Even the rock itself seemed to have disappeared from beneath his boots. He flattened out on the rough surface, resting his chin on his palms, and tried to perfect a strategy for getting rid of his enemy. It would never happen again.

Then, directly in front of his gaze, it seemed just a few inches from his eyes, the Indians began to leap out of the hole. He stiffened. As soon as they had disappeared behind the hillside, he ran down to see where they were going. By the time he reached a point where he could see to the floor of the desert below, the first motor had started up. In pickups, not using headlights, just their parking lights and their knowledge of the road, they disappeared with

- 128 -

flapping tailgates into the south. Tot stood beside Peter and they watched the tops of the trucks swing in a curve and vanish.

On the way home, Peter repeated phrases in her ear: "They grew up and ran out. They got up and flew out. They grew up and ran out."

Peter wondered if the way to kill Shepp would occur to him at the right moment or on a special day. Less than a week after he and Tot saw the Indians, he walked into the place where Shepp worked on the edge of town. But the tall boy wasn't vulnerable in any way. He was fingering a small part that needed to be replaced in his ignition system. After he was through cursing it and had thrown it aside, Peter said, "Turn around, I want to show you something."

"Not now, diddy-doo."

"It's not a trick."

Shepp turned and faced the opposite wall.

"Now stick your tongue out." Peter reached up and tugged at Shepp's thick hair. He had done it to himself many times, trying to understand why the Indians had yanked their hair that way.

"What are you doing?" Shepp demanded, waving his arms.

Now, Peter thought, if he could grab a weapon, he would be able to beat Shepp's skull, but he hadn't thought far enough ahead. "Reach around and pull your hair this way and stick your tongue out."

Shepp turned around and grabbed Peter by the shirt.

"What are you doing?"

"I saw the Indians do it."

"What Indians?"

"There was more than one ..."

Shepp walked away a few steps, then faced him again.

"Where?"

"I saw them do it a few nights ago ... in the tunnel."

"You're lyin' ..."

Shepp walked over to the radio that sat on a shelf and turned the sound up. He grabbed a wrench.

Peter's eyes moved from the wrench in Shepp's fist to the panes of glass at the end of the garage.

The wrench belonged in Peter's hands.

"I'm going to go with you some night. We'll see." Shepp nodded, then ducked down under the wheels of his machine and began to work on the alignment. Nothing would ever be perfect in the joints of his old auto. Peter kneeled down and watched carefully. There was the crucial thing! The steering. Shepp would need a bandage for every part of his body. But it had to be done right. If Tot were in the car ... that would destroy the plan. Shepp's arms were spider-like, wrapped in the turning section of the front end. Inside the chassis, he seemed to be keeping house like a meticulous insect. How to get rid of him without destroying her? And Shepp wasn't the only trouble. Someday, Peter might have to give Tot some rough treatment if she didn't do what he said. Then he would be like his enemy.

"I'll be there tonight," Shepp decided.

"All right."

Though Shepp and Peter waited in the tunnel for more than an hour, the Indians did not appear. Peter showed him the boottracks and gave him a detailed account of what the Indians had done.

"Well," Shepp said, looking around slowly, "some-body was here. Maybe you weren't lying."

Peter realized that the Indians only came on special nights.

"My old man says, if there isn't any liquor, there isn't any Indian," Shepp said. "I don't see any bottles."

Peter walked around slowly and sat down.

"You don't know what nights they're going to do it, do you?" Shepp added. "Maybe I should knock your head against the wall."

Peter thought for a minute. "What for?"

"You tried to kill me once, didn't you? If you had two black eyes, you'd know it too."

Shepp whirled, stamping his foot, then said, "Forget about it, I'm not going to hurt you. Listen to the echo. Haw, haw, haw." After a while, he got tired of listening to the echo and flopped down with his back against the wall of the tunnel. He snapped his foot in rhythm to some internal music. Then he jerked forward and took a pack of cards from the breast pocket of his jacket. They made an angry, ripping noise when he shuffled them. "O.K. We'll wait."

Peter cut the deck and handed the cards back to Shepp. After ten hands, Shepp was bored. He let his cards drop on the floor and dozed. Peter stared at his own fingers, holding the overlapping cards, the faces of the kings looking in opposite directions.

Shepp woke up and made another echo. He lifted his chin and glanced quickly at Peter. "Someday," he declared in a loud tone, "I'm going to kill somebody. Can you get the idea of what it makes me feel like? It isn't going to be funny. The guy just isn't going to get up. He'll lay there like a stiffened mule." Then Shepp got to his feet and flashed his light down the tunnel. "I don't know what I'll do afterwards. It isn't going to be an ordinary fight. You aren't the one I'm going to kill, though. Tonight isn't the night."

To Peter, Shepp's speech about killing someone was crazy. He was the shadow that would drop Shepp flat at the right moment.

"Maybe the guy you're going to kill is already

dead, maybe he was killed a few minutes ago somewhere," Peter said.

"What?" Shepp whirled around then beat both his hands against the wall. He let out a whoop. "You aren't crazy. You say things that just make everybody else crazy. Look ... he isn't dead because I haven't killed him yet." Shepp paused, then began again. "I'm the one, the only one, who's going to kill him, do you understand?"

Peter realized that Shepp didn't actually know what would happen after he killed the person. All the possibilities of it could invade and untangle the connections so that he and Shepp might actually talk about it for a few minutes. But it wouldn't change things. Probably, the Indians had buried people in the hills, so there were skeletons all around them, listening to them. To them, Shepp's talk must sound like a waste of breath.

Soon, they were both tired of waiting. The moon had travelled into the west and filled the hole above the tunnel so that when they climbed out to Shepp's car, it was like stepping up into the white surface of the reflecting moon.

Within a month, Peter's mother and father kept their promise and arranged a different kind of trip for Peter. He was to be instructed at a school forty miles beyond Tucson that was "half hobby, half study." Several of his high school teachers had written home to say that Peter was often sleepy in class. More than once, he had appeared with his pajama bottoms showing beneath his trousers.

Before six weeks had passed, Peter was asked to leave his new school. When he returned home, his father and mother told him to look for a job, saying he would feel less discontented if he was busy on the weekends. It took him a month to find part-time work. His whole life changed. Saturdays and Sundays, he found himself walking along the avenues and alleys of Shays, following his shortcut to work. The pavement, the dirt streets, underwent his careful scrutiny. He tested their surfaces – wondering if, as in the time of the Civil War, there wasn't an underground railroad beneath them. The underground life kept jumping out at him from his history books. There were the catacombs of the early Christians, the cable that ran under the Atlantic ocean and carried people's voices, airplane factories hundreds of feet underground and the bomb shelters that several of the more fearful of Shays' citizens had built beneath the dust.

But no one at the theatre where Peter worked was planning an escape, or preparing for the great journey to freedom.

With a tie wrapped around his neck, sweating in his uniform, Peter stood by an aisle of a movie theatre getting sore feet. When elderly ladies came in, Peter pushed the seats down for them. They, in turn, told the manager what a nice gentleman he had working for him. Actually, what Peter liked best in the theatre were the coverings of the seats which moved beneath his fingers like furry animals.

The manager of the theatre wore strong-smelling pomade and tried to look at his reflection in the little mirrors behind the popcorn concession. He reprimanded Peter every hour or so, because Peter was supposed to be more alert. The scuffles outside

Peter did not have to attend to. But if couples were being "too sloppy" - the manager's term for loud necking - Peter had to find them and shine his flashlight on them. His flashlight usually pointed at the large pastel mural on the ceiling. Although he fixed the backdoor so that Tot could come in and watch the show, he didn't get to see her as much as he wanted.

The hysterics and gunblasts of the features had to compete with the inter-club rivalries in the audience. Peter could seldom hear the dialogue. When the equipment failed, if the manager wasn't around, the girl who sold candy and popcorn worked herself into a frenzy, stepped into the mayhem, and using strong language, told everyone to shut up.

Peter's parents had promised him that after he began to make his own money, he would sleep better. But his sleep didn't improve. Sometimes, he awoke to find that he had unfastened his pajama tops during the night, exposing his chest and throat to the desert air.

After Peter cashed his paychecks, he put the bills

in the back of his drawer. They sat there all folded up. He didn't know what to do with them. But they seemed to be talking to him from the back of his dresser. He decided to buy presents for his friends.

His fingers ran from window to window, without a pause. Nothing in the stores looked good to him.

Then one night the girl behind the candy counter asked him for a favor. She met him at a coffee shop and said she had to leave town to escape someone who was trying to hurt her. Did Peter have any money? She admitted that she would not be able to return it – at least not soon.

Quite cheerfully, Peter went home, cleaned out his drawer and gave her close to ninety dollars. Later on, because of what happened, he wished he had held on to it.

The night before Tot's birthday, Peter was relieved from his job by a sleek staff of youths who were juniors and seniors at the high school. They were mostly tan and blonde and they all looked like nothing but fun had ever happened to them. The Chamber of Commerce had rented the theatre for the night, boxing matches were to be shown and every effort was going to be made to please the customers.

As Peter was leaving through the side door, he saw more youths on the sidewalk. One of them hopped into a car and drove it away from the theatre's entrance. In a second, Peter recognized his father's automobile.

Whatever the exact nature of his calculations: Tot's birthday, the tunnel, and a special surprise for her - all contributed to the single action of his returning to his house at a dead run.

Within a few minutes, he emerged, almost invisible under one of his father's hats. His emblem - hammered out on the lid of a trash can - was gripped firmly under his right arm.

Still running, he directed his feet to the lot where he knew the cars were parked. He spotted his father's automobile and jumped in. The key was in the ignition and the motor was still warm. He pushed the gas to the floor and raced out of the lot - leaving seas of dust behind him, then bounced off the curb, in order to avoid a car just entering the lot, and careened to the left – his foot going up and down like an accordion on the gas pedal. He turned left again, and travelled down the main street. He passed in front of the theatre. The noisy, leaping progress of the automobile attracted attention. Luckily, Peter's father was standing with his back to the street.

Peter did not have complete control of the car. The parking attendant Peter had passed on the way out of the lot, entered the intersection from the right. Peter swerved to the left. The car speeded up, rolled over the curb and travelled a few more yards before smashing into the window of a sporting-goods store. As Peter jumped out of the car, a burglar alarm went off in his ears.

He lifted his hat to see where he was going. In a second, he ran down the alley in the darkness. It took him seven minutes to get home, avoiding all the houses where dogs might bark.

In the dark house, he replaced his father's hat and hid in his bed. He expected the police or some of the people who had seen him to pound on the door.

He tested words, first in his own mind, then aloud, before pressing his face into the pillow and trying to forget what had happened.

For hours, no one came home. At that very minute, Mr. Poole, who had answered the call of his license number, was being cheered up by two men from Phoenix. A conversation had started. Good things were to come from the association and Peter's father - pretty drunk - did not even go outside to inspect the damage but gave twenty dollars to the boy who was going to have the car towed away. He laughed and announced that the insurance company owed him a car. The rates he paid weren't going to be wasted completely and the other men agreed.

Witnesses swore - judging from the strange hat - the incompetent thief was a drunken Indian.

Meanwhile, Peter waited for his parents to return. For certain, his father would burst into the room and swear at him and hit him and make up a punishment that would last forever.

He waited. His mother came home from her card game. His father's footsteps went past his door. In a few minutes, the house was filled with the sound of Mr. Poole's snoring. Toward early morning, Peter fell asleep.

But the next day, Mr. Poole was furious. When he woke up, he looked at his body in the mirror. What kind of a soft creature was he becoming? He decided to reform himself with labor. His careless mood of the night before was transformed by his headache into an attitude of resentment and fury. The men from Phoenix had dropped him off at the house. He didn't have a car to drive to work in the next day. Why did the Indian have to steal his car? He knew other people who deserved to have their cars stolen more than he did. Even though he had insurance, one way or the other, it would end up costing him money. He talked to himself as he walked out to the garage.

Peter woke up and the events of the night before seemed like a dream. At breakfast, his mother described the details of the theft. She watched his face carefully and concluded that his surprise was genuine.

Then, when he went to his room to get dressed for Tot's party, the man's voice pierced the walls - calling to Peter to help him out back.

"Mush head with eight feet, sour toothache, gut bender," Peter muttered. His heart, as though some old bellows had breathed flame into it, grew hot, then cool again. "I'll help a little, then go," Peter thought. If he didn't do some work, his father would make it into a marathon and keep him busy the whole afternoon.

Outside, the old garage had its door flung open and looked as enormous as a train station.

"I'm going to a party in a little while," Peter said, looking up at his father.

"Not this second you aren't. Get in there, straighten some of those boxes out, move some of that stuff back, the rain's been getting to it." The man was unrolling some tar paper to a width of ten feet where he kneeled up on the roof. "Do you know what happened last night?"

"I just heard."

"Isn't that the god-damndest? What do you

think's going to finish this town? Irresponsibility. An impossible bunch of Indians, that's what. And what are you going to do about it?"

"There's a party this afternoon," Peter said again. He paused, then added, "I'll clean up the backyard now." Trying to unscramble the garage would take ages.

Mr. Poole's moustache wiggled and his eyebrows shot up.

"In a hurry, huh?" he grumbled. "Get a holiday to fix a few things and you're all set to run. Think you break your back at that theatre?" Then words followed, endless strings of words. Mostly about payments on the house.

Peter listened for a minute.

Behind the man, like a giant paddleboat stoked so high it billowed in flames, the sun in the sky travelled along in a blind path. Down in the works, stood the sun himself. With long, pencil-thin drooping moustaches and two pistols on his hips, he was shouting orders to his frantic slaves. The moon was present too, but invisible. She cared for Peter and was close enough to see all the things that were taking place on earth. Round and tender, she often stepped to the lonely porch of her white hotel to watch and see. She looked down and wished people better days. She knew the sun, and she said, "One of these days, he's going to be tongue-tied when he finds out, one of these days." Any man who would burn her up in the nighttime and freeze her in the daytime wasn't worth a fig. He wasn't the one who created all those beautiful things on earth. She knew this with her unsatisfied daughters crying behind her in the lonely rooms of the hotel. "One of these days he's going to come out of that engine room and take a look at himself and see what all that blasting and firing away of his has done, and his eyes are going to pop out big as himself, black and ugly, and he'll go down to his boiler room and steer his boat straight at my steps and everything he sees and he'll throw his slaves in too till he's satisfied that nothing's left." That's the way the moon talks. She has her few pleasures and her duties in the air.

And Peter after nodding his head to the words

of his father and listening to the inner whispering, dashed into the garage for a broom. He got busy too. He swept. Then he moved around the yard like a whirlwind, picking up ice cream sticks, bobby pins, leaves – not quite certain where all these things had come from.

Soldier turned moralist, the man on the roof continued to talk with a painful repetition. The rhythm of abuse that seemed to operate in his mind – triggered by the car incident – swung like a whirlpool and gathered in the topic of Shepp. Peter's father, after endless months, returned to the subject he could not get over: the fact that his son had kicked another boy (a damned good football player too) right down a hole and pretended he was a hero for doing it.

Peter ignored the words as the singing of birds is ignored by certain animals when they hunt. His mind was filled with tidal waves. A wooden pointer circled, then tapped a danger area on a map of the West Coast. A teacher in class was describing land faults that no miracle could prevent from one day pitching all the people on the coast into the sea. Asked why the people did not move their houses back from the ocean, the teacher answered, "Move back? Yes, why don't they?"

The voice in the air rose to an insistent pitch and Peter glanced behind him. He could see one of his father's legs hanging down as though the man were going to shove off into a crowd of angels. The angry figure seemed far away and Peter was glad of that.

And from the roof, Peter was like a little magnet – diminishing, magnetized, small, in sympathy with all things humble – stuffing the yard debris into his pockets. Peter had control of the ground. That was his place. His father could have the roof for as long as he wanted it.

The yard was clean. Peter ran into the garage to empty his pockets. Then there was a splash. A tin plate fell, nails sprayed all over the asphalt.

A voice cut through him like iron. "You," it said. Peter's father was dangerously close to him. "You!" A bark. Then a whisper that was harsh and panicked.

His father's eyes were bulging. The little military moustache was a-bristle. Peter rushed out. A vision for the sages unpealed in the bright sunlight. For a moment, the boy froze in a kind of ecstasy.

As though his father were performing exercises – doing his sit-ups – the man was straining to grab his leg. But the leg, like a stump pointing upward, was so far above his waving arms that he couldn't reach it. The iron vane around which his knee was cocked did not look as though it was going to hold for much longer. Should Peter drag out the double-bed so that when his father fell, he would not hurt himself?

Peter strained with his hands to support his father's back but was knocked aside by one of the flailing arms. He ran over to the ladder. But he couldn't set it up fast enough. The ladder was knocked aside, to the ground. Peter set the ladder against the garage again and hurried up the rungs to the roof. With a terrible noise, the weather vane gave way. Mr. Poole flopped to the cement. His motion caused him to end up on his face.

There it was. Peter was certain that below him, the ultimate doom had befallen his father. He sat like a little dog on the roof, arms locked straight while he gazed down. His knees shifted on the sun-softened tar.

Peter's muscles twitched as though he had been doing strenuous exercise. He crouched lower. He wanted to look at, but did not want to touch the form that was so quiet for a change.

His mother appeared at the back door. She was humming in her throat, pretending she didn't care what the men were doing outside. Then she saw her son, up there in the sky, and following his gaze, saw what looked like a pile of clothing.

She hurried out, wearing her usual smile that anticipated disappointment, every part of her wiggling with its own idea of how it should cross the yard.

She kneeled beside her husband, then jumped back as though the form had bitten her. She stared up at Peter. "Aren't you going to come down?" Then she hurried back into the house.

He remained. Every footfall of hers was like a

fossil's impression on his mind.

He looked at the town. He could see Tot's house, the only two-story dwelling in view. Nothing seemed to be moving. The sun was still high and there were few shadows. He was cooked. The town was. His father was. Peter felt a boiling in his brain. Certainly his chin would weigh him down until he would fall beside his motionless father.

Siren grinding, a white ambulance travelled backwards up the drive.

Two men gathered Mr. Poole and gently placed him on a stretcher.

"Is he all right? Tell me so I'll know. Will he be all right?" Mrs. Poole was dancing around the men.

"Can't say, Missus. I reckon he hurt his teeth, might have broke some ribs too. Are you going to ride with him?"

"Were you up there, Peter?" she said, squinting at him, shading her eyes with her hand.

Peter shook his head.

She ducked into the van of the ambulance. As it pulled away, the boy realized he had missed his chance to go along. If he wanted to see his father at the hospital, he would have to walk.

The sign of the theatre where Peter worked blinked on and off in the daylight. Noticing it now, the only movement in the city, it occurred to him that if he had stood in his uniform by the aisle door he might have been at a convenient distance from his father's mishap. Then he could have gone to Tot's house, straight from the theatre, without having to worry about his father.

Whatever celebration was being enjoyed at Tot's now, it seemed out of bounds, as though taking place on a different shore.

The palms of his hands were sticky from the tar paper. He rubbed them with his fingers, then climbed slowly down the ladder.

Peter wandered around the yard, found himself walking along the street. The holiday had emptied it.

Soon his thumb was drifting behind him as he walked backwards along the highway. No one stopped to pick him up. After he had walked a ways along the mine road, all the blackness and denial of his locked room, the theatre, his uniform – faded behind him.

Half way down the ladder, Peter paused, then – while examining the floor of the tunnel – he slowly continued to the bottom. More people had been to the passageway, but not Indians. In four places, perfect squares had been cut into the floor, about half a foot deep. Little metal trays sat nearby, filled with stones and bits of metal. Who had dug the holes and why were they surrounded by lines of string? The paper had said a professor might come out to study the tunnel, but it looked like it would be turned into a jumble.

Peter looked at all the objects in the trays. His face felt hot.

The spirit of change was there, inescapable.

He walked to the opposite end of the passageway and sat down with his back against the tiles. He slept with a round gold object in his hand.

When he opened his eyes, it was dark except for the moonlight coming in through the distant hole. Then a figure leaped to the floor. They were jumping down the hole like broken parts of the same long fencepost. He heard one of them curse. A long growl, but different from a dog's, stopped suddenly. Flashlight beams crisscrossed on an animal that made an attempt to rush through them, then backed away. They surrounded it and took off their belts. A coyote – probably coming down through a different opening in the hillsides –had found its way to the floor of the tunnel. The Indians began to howl. Owwwww. Owwwww. They seemed to be having fun with it. In the beams of their flashlights, the animal's yellow hair was chopped and scissored while they tied it up in a halter of wide belts. Its legs dug in the air while they lifted the coyote high, the head wrapped twice and the lips shut tight with the leather. It twisted with its neck and spine, but instead of the growls, there were whines. The suffocated noises grew fainter as the Indians jumped over the lines of string, kicking some of the stakes aside, and disappeared into the orifice of the oval room.

Peter waited, sweat cooling his forehead. Then

he crept forward until he could see the men through the opening of the room. Their clothes were in a pile against the wall and they were sitting in a circle again. Did they believe what they were saying to each other? One of the men – before he went down the hole – had something to eat in his hand; he didn't want to give it up. He took a few quick swallows, then shoveled it into the mouth of another Indian before the wave motion passed through him and he pushed himself into the hole.

Behind them, its coat reflecting the firelight, the animal lay on its side, moving from time to time and making a low sound.

Peter went back to his hiding place. In about a half hour, they came down the length of the tunnel. A thin trickle of saliva moistened the walls of his throat.

They were gone. With a boiling in his head, Peter returned to the oval room and leaned over the pit; in echoing shapes, the rooms and stones of the hills reared above him – now an elaboration of his brain. He could feel himself falling. Once more he turned and lost himself in the curving ways beneath the earth. For a while, he felt glad. But he knew his spirit would continue to live in the feathery darkness until he could stay with Tot always in some place on the surface of the earth.

When he woke up, he knew the Indians were no longer there, but he heard sounds like their voices. It was the voice that had been built into the hills themselves.

He climbed the ladder and started down the mine road. The sun was halfway across the sky. It was already a full day since his father had fallen from the roof.

Just as he reached the main highway, he saw someone approaching him. At first, the person in the distance was no bigger than a can of soup. Then the figure transformed itself into a boy almost exactly Peter's size. But he didn't walk right. He walked as though he was about to kneel at every step. The wind blew dust against his arms. It was the boy that everyone laughed at. Peter wondered what to make of his head. The odd figure said hello – and as usual – his tongue clicked before he spoke. Then he turned back and glanced at Peter sidelong. The base of his neck seemed to have been sewn into the top of his shirt; maybe he was the result of one of the bomb tests or an experiment at the hospital in Tucson. Peter watched him plod along between the margin of the road and the tall bushes that had been planted as dust screens by the highway department. He was afraid if he stared too hard, part of the cootie-boy would work up into his own system. Then the strange individual turned to face Peter again. The staring, on this particular day, seemed to bother him. He stooped, picked up two stones and threw them hard in Peter's direction. They winged past his shirt, directly into a wooden post of a sign that stood not two feet away. The wood doubled the sound of the rocks and they fell harmlessly among the ice-white bits of gravel on the roadside. The boy's tongue seemed wedged in the side of his mouth as he faced his likeness on the road. Then he continued on his journey. The wood of the sign tolled the sounds like a clock. Peter felt as though two invisible pins had entered his body and stayed there.

Within a few days, Peter's father was back from the hospital, but the boy was convinced that somehow, his father was really dead. A black and blue mark like an X could be seen on the bridge of Mr. Poole's nose and one of his teeth was chipped.

Peter was no closer to solving the problem of how he was going to get rid of his enemy. The conflict went on in silence. Never touching, they wore each other down.

After a while, Peter got sick and had to stay in bed. He occupied the hours with reading and made up his own version of certain things Tot had told him to read.

On the first day he stayed home from school, because he was coughing and unable to breathe, Tot had come to the house and handed him an underlined copy of the Bible and instructed him to memorize the underlined parts. He had read them, but after ten chapters, had put the Book aside and hunted around for a pencil. Whatever the rest of the Bible was like, he decided the beginning part couldn't be

- 157 -

the truth. Lifting the covers over his shoulder, clamping a notebook against his stomach, he began to write down his own ideas.

While he was working one afternoon, his mother came into his room with a gloomy expression on her face. Beneath her dark slacks, she was wearing white shoes and black socks.

"All right, Peter. You did it," she said after staring at him for a minute. Her voice was somewhere between a croon and a whine.

"Did what?"

She rocked back and forth from foot to foot as though trying to decide whether or not to tell him. Then she marched into the kitchen.

Peter kicked his way out of the covers and followed her. She was pale, and blue around the eyes.

"Did what?"

The newspaper sat on the table in front of her and her finger was moving across a column. Every day she studied the news. Catastrophes caused by acts of God were inevitable, but there were worse things. The murders and bombings by people who didn't have to do it – those were the items that made her afraid. Anyone – no matter what he looked like – could be guilty. Peter had set off a fire alarm and kicked another boy down a hole and she had no idea what he was going to do next. She tried to keep him nearby, either in the house or on a strict schedule. But she failed. He escaped her watchful stare and went where he wanted. She felt certain that one day, because of her inability to control him, he would jump out at her from the newsprint. He would have committed an act, like the ones that made her rise from the kitchen table, chewing her lips. It would be like looking at herself in a mirror that showed its opposite.

"Get back into bed, Peter. You have a fever."

"What did I do?"

"You know that better than I do ... if you did it. It's nothing we can talk about, so get back into bed."

As his mother looked at the arms extending beneath the sleeves of his faded pajamas, it seemed impossible to her that Peter could be responsible for the girl's pregnancy. No, the cause of her gloom had not been printed in a newspaper column – yet.

Her whole body and her expression communicated a terrible wrath to Peter; he was happy to get back into bed. She didn't mean the incident with his father. She didn't mean that he had pushed his father off the roof, because Mr. Poole had told her the exact details three times.

Peter recounted to himself all his evil deeds and in doing so, found he was completely unable to work. He had to go to sleep and wake up again before he could concentrate.

Nothing more about it was said for two days. Mrs. Poole didn't know whether to call the girl's mother, or try to make arrangements herself for a foster home, or possibly offer money. Dimly, she still dreamed that her husband would be able to cope with Peter. But when he failed, she felt unable to do anything either. Mr. Poole had never really achieved a triumph over his son. His rage made her doubt that he ever would. Pregnancy was a female problem. If the man found out about it, he would probably demolish her favorite piece of furniture. And she was afraid that he might hurt Peter. No, she would wait and see what happened.

But after two days she walked into his room with a screwdriver in her palm and ordered him to get out of bed.

"Why?" he said.

"Just get out of bed. The doctor's coming and I want you to take the lock off your door. You don't know what he might think if he sees that we lock you in sometimes. He might start a rumour about us. Who knows? Will you untighten the screws now! I'll try to do the rest. The latch on the window too. Hurry up."

Peter got out of bed, took the screwdriver and twisted the silver heads until they came out of the wood. He got back into bed, and within ten minutes, there were two enormous exits in his room. A door and a window. Anything might wander in or out.

"You're just lucky I feel sorry for you," she said, tapping the iron of the tool against her palm.

What was in store for him, Peter wondered. She

was just trying to scare him.

She had begun to review the things that had happened during the past months and was beginning to suspect that he could be the one who had driven the car through the window of the sporting goods store. Anything could happen. In her more foreboding moments, she could imagine him eating, like a termite, the wooden supports that were weakening in the garage. After reading about a Peruvian earthquake that tumbled dozens of villages, she wondered if he hadn't mumbled a formula in his room. Not too many nights before, in a dream, his spirit appeared to her in the form of a silver-toothed beaver that said, "You'd better figure me out."

The doctor arrived and tried to scare Peter too. He left him with a bottle of pills. The name on the label was so long that Peter was certain the doctor had made it up. The boy wanted to ignore all these frightening portents and concentrate on his work. But his fever remained high.

He began to think that all the pills, shots and syrups might not save him. He decided he had better take what he had written of his book and walk over to Tot's house and give it to her. His teeth were sore, his eyes almost shut with his drawn-out fever. His limbs felt shaky and quivery. He had been in bed too long. The unresponsive walls, the sounds from the kitchen, blurred voices, the television set at night, all worked on his imagination to confirm the possibility of a swift and anonymous death.

He made the decision while he ate his dinner. A small red cloud kept him company. It seemed to be hoarding the failing light – like a bird which had been sent from a different world to take away the rays of the sun. In return, it had dumped out on the earth the distant houses and wires that Peter could see from his bed.

He pretended he had swallowed his pills, and feigned sleep when his mother came in to take away his food. No words were spoken. His parents went to bed early, and after an hour's wait, Peter crept out the front door. So shaky did he feel, he knew if he hopped out of the window, he might fall down. But in the cold night air, watery arms and legs became shivering flesh again. He was glad to see the sleeping houses, the street lamps, which for some reason had not been turned on that night, and above them, stars gathering like fleas.

"Are you all better?" Tot asked from her window; a voice from the dark house whose owner Peter could not make out. "I'll meet you downstairs. Come to the front door."

She was standing on the step, the door ajar behind her.

"I've been writing this book," Peter said. "I wanted you to see it. Maybe you'll like it. Keep it."

"You're not all better yet?"

"No."

"I don't think I can let you in, then."

"That's O.K. Here. Take it." His teeth chattered.

She reached out her hand and took the unfastened pages. Then she turned and Peter heard them drop behind her on the floor.

"What did you do that for?"

"O.K........" She thought for a minute. "Peter,

you'd better come in."

"You said...."

"No. That's all right. I thought if I came over to see you –" and her breath stopped as though she had just stepped into water.

Then her breath came again. The door swung open and Peter was being drawn inside. "I was afraid you might get me sick, Peter."

She took his hands and pressed them against her stomach, but a heavy woolen covering was in the way and he didn't know what she wanted.

"What's going on?"

He heard her feet step along the thin rug, then she turned on a light.

A brightly colored afghan was wrapped around her shoulders, the edges touching the floor. She held out the corners. She seemed to be prepared for a long journey.

"Now do you see?"

"No."

She shook her head and was silent.

Peter thought he was still in a dream. He had

awakened her by throwing stones at her window. Now she was trying to make him play a game in her dream. He went back to the door and began to pile up the scattered pages, thinking that he would have to find someone else to give them to. He felt like going to sleep. He walked over to the couch and set the little book behind him on a table, then slumped down on the cushions.

"Last night, I didn't think I'd get well," he said. "But I feel pretty good now. Now that I'm walking around I feel all right. I wanted to see you again. The doctor said if the fever kept getting higher, I'd be finished."

"Well, I won't tell you until I'm sure you're going to get better. You'll die a lot happier if you don't know."

"What?"

She sat on the couch directly to his left and covered her feet with the afghan.

"First of all, Mother says we're going to move out of Shays."

An alarm drilled. He sat up. "What?"

"Don't get mad. I don't know, Mother says she wants to move soon."

"What's going on?"

"Do you tell me everything?"

"Almost …. Sure."

"I haven't been in school for three days. I've just been sitting here. Mrs. Bright drove me home from the nurse's office."

"What's wrong with her?"

"She's mad … because I'm going to have a baby."

Peter looked at Tot's stomach again and put his hands against it. Definitely bigger. Then he gazed around the room. There, to behold, in an aquarium were the electric blue fish Tot's mother had to feed all the time, the tall, milk-white vase stood on another table and behind it was the big chest of drawers with a carved mirror above it … But Peter felt like he was on a moving train, being hustled away from all the things he had ever wanted. She had told him good news, about the baby. At the same time she announced she was leaving. Soon, it would all be over. The world was getting the best of him. Peter decided he might as well be sitting on top of a mountain as in the foreign space filled with all the vanishing objects.

Her hands were so warm that his felt cool by comparison. She pressed them hard. Especially now that she had said the words, she was certain Peter would accept the baby. It seemed for a moment that wringing his hands would succeed in drawing from him a word or expression affirming that things were all right.

But he sat back, grabbing at his legs, and became more and more gloomy.

"You can't," he said. What moved outside, what invisible shadow was forcing itself between him and Tot? Only now, when he was sick, did it make itself known. Why was she moving away?

"Now, when I tell you what happened, you look like you don't trust me, Peter."

But his misery and confusion, which she could see, caused her to stop hoping for the moment. He wasn't warmly dressed and she covered him with the afghan.

"My mother said you'd get mad. I'll bet you're sorry she didn't come down to talk to you."

"I'm not sorry," Peter said. It seemed to him that Tot's mother was the true cause of his unhappiness.

Also in his mind the thought turned, that if he hadn't taken the job like his father told him to, he might have been more careful and she wouldn't be in such a fix.

"We have to get out of here."

"How, Peter?"

"We have to get out of here. Both of us."

"How can I come with you?" Peter was silent.

"You really want to be the father?"

"What do you mean?" he asked.

"I told you before ....." she began.

He closed his hand over her mouth, then pushed her back on the couch. "I am the father."

He wished he hadn't given his money to the girl at the theatre. There were other regrets, and questions too.

"But you're sick, Peter," Tot said. Then she

kissed him.

The kisses, the belief that Peter still loved her, that he was going to understand - all worked upon her a temporary relief.

But in his own bed, the uninhabited land outside the lines of her explanations became busy with doubts. Days passed, his fever dropped, yet his mind became raw and would not be satisfied. Somewhere, an enemy wandered. Peter could not ignore him. He must track him down. How the shadow, even fleetingly had passed over him, he could not understand. Through Tot, Peter now lived a life that was stripped to the bone.

Weeks would have to pass before he would have enough money to travel a long way. Perhaps he would have to go with her as far as Chicago. The sea roared in his sleep, moving at a gallop; it crossed the turning sand, sliding under the doorways of those who were to be swept away - never to return again. There had to be a plan. Often, his ears remembered the sound of papers, falling carelessly behind her, just at the time he thought he had to say good-bye.

Then, the windy night before he was to return to school, he stood in his room, buttoning and pulling over himself as many clothes as he could possibly wear. Shirts, pajamas, trousers, a light and heavy jacket. He filled his pockets with all the things he wanted.

Moonlight found its way into the house through wind-scratched panes. Peter thought that stealing money from his father, vanishing as quickly as dust, would put him out of the range of the brainless forces that were closing in from all sides. Some day he would return. No one would recognize him. A glint would reflect from his body. He would speak with the voice of a cave. From the host of the town would be surrendered his enemy. All would be forgiven.

He tiptoed into his father's room. On the floor, he could make out his father's trousers where the man had stepped out of them before falling onto the cot. Peter could expect to find at least twenty, perhaps as many as fifty dollars in the chain clasp his father carried. He bent down to the trousers and lifted out the clip that held the money.

Then Peter's feet came to a stop. The sound of breathing blew in his ears and reassured him that the man was still asleep. But on the cot, poking up from the pillow above the covers, was something other than his father's face. The man's features had been completely changed. It now looked like the rear end of a man. Naked buttocks. Pressures, which for their sea-force must have come from a different world, had expanded the cheeks to three times their size. The nose and mouth had become a single line dividing the head from top to bottom. Peter rubbed his own head. Now he could see how far the corruption of his father's flesh had progressed. The whole world had changed. Then a sound came from the cot. The face moved slowly, moaned as in agony. Peter's hand flew out, gesturing to stop it. Backing out of the room, he turned and left the house.

A wind drew up the dust in the night, tugged at the sage, and gathering force, swept down the deserted streets, opening and closing the screens.

Peter strode through the cold night. Ahead of him on the road, the wind blew the dust in long weary lines that vanished in the darkness. Clouds blew over, sand and later rain stung his cheeks. Lost for a while, his feet striking rocks and sage, he was trying to find the road in the dark. Just when he thought he had found it, just when he thought his hands were pressing the thorn-sharp concrete, his foot caught beneath a soft weight, a body no longer alive but not yet stiff. From the trousers, which he remembered, and the size of the form, Peter knew it was the boy who had thrown the stones at him not many weeks before. The shirt seemed too elaborate now, as though the body's interior had become the shirt in the act of violence which must have occurred within the hour. As Peter could read for himself the next day and the day after, a Grey-hound bus had struck the boy, and hurled his soul to whatever star or sea receives the souls of the dead.

Without thinking, Peter removed the shirt and replaced it with one of his own; then added his long coat with the deep pockets. He exchanged trousers and shoes with him, even while the still potent muscle of the wind spun the tears from his eyes and carried them in the direction of the storm. Peter loved this person now more than he had loved his father who was still sleeping at the house. Before, the boy had seemed ugly. Now he looked like a mysterious fragment that - once destroyed - was beautiful. Again, the whole world had changed.

Thirty feet away, in the branches of a bush, he found the head. He was almost sure he could hear it singing. But how do you sing when your head is no longer a part of your body? Perhaps the boy's head had not been suited to his body in the first place. Without a stutter anymore, or a click of the tongue, it sang all the way along the road to the tunnel. At the foot of the ladder, Peter buried it, where no one would look for it and everyone jumped down.

The next morning, ninety miles from the town of Shays, Peter worried what Tot must be thinking. Not telling her he was alive would be cruel; it would more than repay her for how she had treated his book. How long could she keep his secret? For a little while, she would have to live without assurances. From minute to minute, anything could take place. Maybe he'd be gone for a long time, but he'd have to be totally dead until he was old enough or smart enough to show up again. Then what would she say? She'd know for certain that the dead are a lot crueler than the living. It would be as though he were the leaves of a hundred winters, arriving in a wild heap, but more splendid and solemn. She would remember his death and yet, see him walking! Even he didn't know the hiding place from which he'd emerge or what would break loose like crumbling earth when he appeared again, like a reawakened creature from under the ground.

In fact, when Tot heard the news of his death, she ran out in the street and expected to see him. She went to his house and searched for him in his room. The she cried and – still not knowing what to believe – turned and went back to her home.

Peter had come to see. To see what would happen.

He had popped up in the world and made his gestures and had helped to uncover the ancient city. He came and witnessed it. That was enough.

But Tot needed time to think the thing out and see her part in it. She demanded a sound. She wanted his voice to come singing. But how do you sing when your head no longer belongs to your body? Your head rolls in the dust and the stars look down and you open your mouth and sing as you go.

PETER'S TESTAMENT

I want back the tree, the rock, and the ruby. I will never make them again the same way if they disappear because nothing has ever been made the way I wanted it. I couldn't control it. When I was left alone at first I didn't know what had happened. I was too heartsick to understand what was wrong. The first thing I did was I opened my mouth and that's when I found out I didn't have one. I found out I didn't have any eyes or feeling. I might have left everything alone if it hadn't been for those things I couldn't feel any more. Inside me now, there was nothing I could do or feel but my own thoughts. A part of me was far away by that time – dancing around and putting himself out so he couldn't be seen in the darkness. And that's when thoughts began to fly from my mind like all kinds of razor blades.

My old self turned around, brilliant like fire. He felt my thoughts like stabs in the back. But he didn't make any answer. And he never answered in a way I would listen to until I made the sky. But a tree is an answer, a rock is, and so is the ruby.

"So," he finally said, from his house in the black water at the bottom of the sea, "You won't let me be happy. If I'm selfish, why are you trying to make me look like you, why are you stabbing me with your thoughts and trying to make me perfect?"

"If you let go, I'll make you perfect in a second," I said, and that's all I would say then.

And as I set to work at it, every inch and atom and minute became a war because he had a hold on my mind. Everything became a trap and held my mind this way and that way, but never the right way. But I have a trick that makes me stronger.

And I never had a finger to harm. I have to crawl inside of things and have to watch them dodge past me even when they're looking for me and I'm looking for them. Without saying a word.

Then, when it got going, when snails had to eat little plants, and birds, snails, and humans had to eat animals and die themselves, my old part thought he was safe because he said, "Hah, see, you thought you could defeat me by growing things. But you stalk around the earth and when things don't go the way you want them to, you let them die, all because you want them to be just like yourself. You expect the mountain and the ice cream machine to come up to your standard. You curse me because you're the one who wants to live forever. But your method has tricked you. Everything that dies imitates me and wants to take a rest from you like me, and so they want to die too and get their freedom, like me!"

And I said, "That's a lie. There wouldn't have

been anything to die with if you had not left me."

But he creates a great echo in which my words can not be heard. It sounds the other way. "I will kill everything if it doesn't turn out the way I want it to."

"See, I can mock you anytime," he says.

Then I was tired of him and told him, "I only want there to be love. You make humans from the forest think they are different from humans in the desert, and you make them laugh at one another because of the places where they come from and different temperatures and hair styles and tallness, and so you die with them every time they ignore me. Do not mock at me. Your selfishness is in everything that grows, and in the heart too. I can see it in the heart of the person who has a favorite and will not let anyone else come near, in the heart of the person who wants his family to win everything and nobody else's. All this makes you glad, but you know you can't defeat me. Let go because you are too selfish for me. I want to go fast and you won't let me. You blind me and so it is you who curses yourself. Everything dies, as you say, but I know you don't care. I will gladly give everything to you if you will not resist me."

Then he tried to answer.

And that's the way it happens every minute.

THE END